REDRUM

Bad Family
1st edition
(First German edition)
Copyright © 2019
(First American edition)
Copyright © 2019
REDRUM BOOKS, Berlin
Publisher: Michael Merhi
Translated by Simon Kossov
Editor: Monica J. O'Rourke
Proofreading: Jasmin Kraft
Cover design and concept:
MIMO GRAPHICS by using an
illustration by Shutterstock

ISBN: 978-3-95957-549-2

e-mail: merhi@gmx.net
www.redrum-verlag.de

YouTube: Michael Merhi Books

Facebook page: REDRUM BOOKS

Facebook group:

REDRUM BOOKS - Nichts für Pussys!

SIMONE TROJAHN
BAD FAMILY

About the Book

What does family mean to you? Warmth, security, solidarity?

Then you haven't yet met the Kollers …

Seventeen-year-old Fips and his siblings have hardly known what a normal family is. Living with a sadistic father and an insensitive mother is a nightmare of oppression and violence.

Through the years, the domineering head of the family has succeeded in completely instrumentalizing his own family and degrading his children to henchmen of his cruel crimes.

Fips also commits unspeakable atrocities under his father's guidance. By the time he finally finds the strength to fight his demons, time is running out.

Will the boy succeed in saving his father's victims as well as his own soul, or is it already too late?

About the Author

Simone Trojahn writes terrifying, realistic, profoundly ruthless fiction. This exceptional author has been in the social sector for many years and knows the dark sides of life. In a unique way, she shows what happens if we become the person we never wanted to be.

SIMONE TROJAHN

BAD FAMILY

Thriller

Preface

Dear readers:

The book you are about to read had a short life after its first publication. I'd received positive feedback from some who read about this monstrous family the first time around, for which I would like to express my sincere gratitude.

The book has been given a new robe and a new polish. Many thanks to my editor, Stefanie Maucher, who was so quick and helpful and gave all her heart to this project.

Here are a few words about the story and its origins:

Time and again we hear in the media about terrible deeds that are committed not only by one person but by several or even by a group. I always wonder how it was possible for multiple people to gather at the same time and place, all with the same cruel intentions, seemingly without conscience. Is wickedness contagious? Or are they just followers who do not dare stand against the culprits? And how can these culprits be so sure everyone will do as they say? How do they know who they can reveal their perfidious plans to - and to whom they shouldn't?

These considerations led me to the question of what the whole thing would be like in a family into which the future perpetrators would first be born as victims. Can evil be learned and taught? Or is it inevitable as a member of such a family? How difficult would it be for an individual to stand up to the rest of the family?

Can you develop a conscience in such a poisoned environment? Is blood always thicker than water?

Personally, I think it would be tremendously difficult to avoid such a fate. You'd have to have a special heart and an incredibly strong character. Can you even develop such strength if you grew up in such conditions?

I would say partially, but not completely. One would probably not survive without a black spot on the soul. And a bit of a monster will always remain.

I hope to give you some food for thought with the story about Fips's fight against the windmills of his own kinship. First and foremost I wish you—as always—some exciting entertainment.

Enjoy the trip into my dark world, and don't forget to gasp for breath while reading.

Prologue
"Only a Memory"

You have to be quiet.
Completely silent.
It won't be so bad then.
Hold your breath and just be quiet ...

Philip, whom everyone calls Fips, presses his dirty little hands to his mouth. He knows his sister is right. He must do as she says.

Be still ... stay quiet ... don't provoke him any further ...

It's so hard!

He is so scared!

Matthias said there are rats down here, bigger than puppies. And spiders. Black and hairy.

Like in the big green book about the jungle that Mama keeps on the living room shelf. Fips has flipped through it often enough. On one side is a huge tarantula that looks like a monster, holding a little mouse in its claws. If you look closely, you can see the drops of blood seeping out of its delicate rosy skin.

How often did Fips wonder if the baby mouse in the photo was already dead?

Was it in much pain?

Did it have a mother who mourned it?

A family?

Here in the darkness, Fips can't stop thinking about the poor little mouse.

It's just like him: delicate, sensitive, and filled with fear.

Trembling, he presses his back against the rough wall and wraps his arms around his knees. Sobs come out of his throat.

Quiet! Shhh! You gotta be quiet! That's what Fanny had said.

His big sister, who had been locked in the old potato cellar in the past. For two days. She's learned her lesson, she says. Fips doesn't really understand why he can't learn like his siblings. Why does it happen to him again and again?

Last time it was so long they'd had to splash water in his face to wake him up. Thirst, hunger, and fear had made him so dizzy and tired in the end that he lay down on the hard ground and just wanted to sleep— or die. Until Dad came and carried him upstairs. Mama cried. She rarely did that. Fips didn't care. He was just happy to finally be back up in the house. He swore it was the last time.

Until it happened again.

But he was only curious and wanted to know what was in the attic, which the kids were not allowed to enter. Only Dad and Andreas, Fips's eldest brother, climb up there regularly, and they always smirk when they come back down. They have a different smell then. Recently they took Matthias with them for the first time, and he looked weird when he came back.

Dad said he's a man now. Whatever that means. Fips doesn't understand. Why do you have to go to the attic to become a man? Besides, Matthias is only sixteen and still looks like a boy.

But Matthias goes to the attic often.

Sometimes alone.

Despite the prohibition, Fips sneaked upstairs because the curiosity was too strong. He had been caught promptly and sent down to the potato cellar again.

Last time he was there, Dad didn't let him out until bathing day. Fips knows the water from the pipe is valuable. His father talks about it all the time. That's why the tub is only filled once a week, and then everyone has to take a bath.

One after the other.

In the same water.

First the parents and then the five children.

Fips and his sister Mitzi (whose real name is Maria) are the youngest and therefore the last to take their turn, and the water is already brown and full of soaked skin scales. Fips finds it disgusting, and he'd refuse if he didn't know what was waiting for him if he did. Mitzi is only nine and still splashes around in a good mood. Sometimes she has to vomit after bathing, and eight-year-old Fips wonders if he's the only one who sees a link here, but at the moment his thirst is so big that he would even drink the bathwater. Besides, he's all aching. Dad beat him with the belt on his back and buttocks until he could hardly stand.

After that, Fips had to go down to the basement.

Why did he do it anyway? He could have guessed that they would catch him.

Dad and Andi are really alert. Nothing goes unnoticed.

In fact, it was Matthias who had grabbed him by the ears to drag him to Dad. Because of him, he sits here in the darkness and almost shits his pants in fear. A little eight-year-old boy who should be outside. With friends. Cycling and climbing trees. Playing soccer and jumping over streams.

He never did all that.

Dad doesn't want him to be a normal kid. After school, he always has to go home straightaway. He has no friends because the other children consider him weird. That's how he smells and looks, with his clothes from the eighties and the ridiculous cooking-pot hairdo Mama cuts for him. He is not one of them. Neither here nor there. He feels as strange in his family as he does at school. Nobody thinks like he does. Nobody understands him.

So he's back in the basement with the low ceiling and the damp walls. Fips doesn't see them, but he knows they're here: Spiders and beetles, slaters and bugs. They scurry through the darkness and will crawl over his hands when he least expects them. Fips barely dares to lean against the wall because he fears that something might crawl onto his body. Something bustling, black, with claws, without eyes. Something so ugly and disgusting that you don't want to imagine it.

Dad says he's a wimp. Matthias also thinks so. Even Mitzi laughs at him. Only Fanny comforts him sometimes and presses his face against her soft breasts.

Then he can hardly breathe, but he still likes it and hopes that she will never let him go.

If Fanny were here, it wouldn't be so bad. She would make him forget the crawling creatures. But she's not here (Dad never would have allowed that), so Fips can only sit on the floor, trembling, holding his mouth shut and thinking of her words.

You have to be quiet.

Completely silent.

It won't be so bad then.

Hold your breath and just be quiet ...

That's what Fips wants to do. For his sister and for himself. And he vows that this will be the last time. He will be a good boy from now on. Just like his brothers.

Suddenly something tickles his neck. Fips raises his hands and screams his head off.

He hears Dad's heavy footsteps and the squeaking of the trap door. Fanny had warned him, but he wouldn't listen.

And now it's getting worse. Dad will come and undress him, so that his body will be just as naked and helpless as that of the baby mouse in the clutches of the tarantula.

He knows he's making it worse, but instead of finally being quiet, Fips screams even louder, his mouth wide open ...

The Time of Their Lives

Susan raised her beer mug and smiled at the young man on the other side of the table. She was still surprised at how heavy the jugs were, though this was her third one, and her head felt like a gas-filled balloon.

They clinked their glasses.

"Prost!"

"Prost," she repeated.

Another new word. She had learned quite a lot in Germany, but never before had she learned such funny expressions like at the Oktoberfest.

They called it *Wiesn* here.

The young man grinned, and Susan grinned back.

The dizziness didn't bother her.

He looked pretty in his leather pants and checkered shirt. His sister was just as pretty in her green dirndl dress, which showed much more neckline than Susan's, who had bought hers in a shop in Munich's pedestrian zone. Excessively overpriced, for sure, but you're only here once.

She didn't like the other brother very much.

He also wore traditional clothing and was just as attractive, but there was something in his eyes that made you feel uncomfortable if you looked at him too long.

Didn't Clara notice?

Susan watched her friend flirt with the man. She leaned excessively forward over the table and let him feed her pieces of pretzel. She was drunk. They all were. The beer tent had been crowded to the limit by lunchtime. The security didn't let anyone else in.

The atmosphere was relaxed. So far, Susan had only experienced something comparable on Mallorca. Many people stood on the benches now, swaying and bawling along with the primitive party songs, which Susan didn't like very much. But after two mugs of beer, it was a bit different. The atmosphere had gripped her in the end. The alcohol caused a pleasant feeling in her belly and head. The colors of the world appeared warmer and stronger than usual in her slightly blurred field of vision. Life was always more exciting and colorful far from home.

Together with her best friend, Clara, she had been on a world trip for almost two months now. During this time they had already seen so much that Susan could only imagine how much more was waiting. It was an impressive, exciting time they would tell their grandchildren about.

The time of their lives.

They had planned four months for it. After that, Susan would study medicine, and Clara would take a job in her father's stock trading company. Life was about to get serious. They would earn money and perhaps start families.

But what was happening here and now they would remember forever and talk joyfully about even years later—like the Oktoberfest and the neat boys in traditional costumes whom they had met there.

Meanwhile, Clara had climbed half over the beer table and snogged with the man whose gaze Susan didn't like. His siblings wanted to clink their glasses again.

Susan raised her mug and drank.

After all, this was the best time of her life, and it would be a sin to waste even a minute of it with gloomy thoughts.

***

An hour later they staggered to the toilet together. Susan had to support her friend. Clara could hardly stand.

She would have liked to talk to her. Alone. At least for a moment. But she didn't have the opportunity, because Fanny, the sister of the two boys, had insisted on accompanying them. Susan couldn't stop admiring her artful up-style hairdo. Small white flowers were embedded in the lush reddish-brown hair. In Bavaria, probably every girl knew how to create such works of art, but Susan still was amazed. She doubted this would be possible with her thin, straight hair. Without being aware of it, she approached Fanny in the bathroom to ask her about it.

Fanny just laughed and made a kissing sound.

Had she even understood Susan?

It was always assumed that everyone in the world was proficient in English, but maybe that was a bit presumptuous.

The younger brother, who'd had his eye on Clara, spoke quite acceptable English. He'd told Susan and

Clara that they were siblings from a small village outside Munich.

Andi, the older one Susan had been bonding with, was rather silent and didn't seem to understand everything she said, although she tried to speak slowly and clearly.

It was similar with Fanny. She looked friendly and sweet but didn't really seem to know what Susan wanted from her.

Maybe they should have learned a little more German before they got here. The communication had definitely been better in Berlin. Of course, they hadn't gotten drunk there at the biggest folk festival in the world.

The noise from the beer tent was still deafening back here in the toilet. Not a good place for conversation. Susan would have liked to have a quiet moment alone with her friend. It was time to talk.

Clara's flirt, Matthias, had already asked whether they would like to go home with them afterward to have a little party. Susan was skeptical, despite how nice the three seemed to be. There was still Matthias's unsteady gaze and the tummy rumbling that he caused in her. It was inexplicable, but nevertheless it was there.

When Susan saw her friend stumbling out of one of the cabins with tangled hair and a reddened face, she realized a reasonable conversation was not possible at the moment.

Fanny laughingly put one hand around Clara's waist and winked at Susan. Susan didn't know how to react, so she tried to dispel her concerns, smiled, and went back to the table with her. The boys had already ordered the next round of beers.

Susan suddenly didn't feel like drinking anymore. The pleasant feeling gradually disappeared. This time she only sipped from her mug when Andi clinked glasses with her.

Clara suddenly sat on Matthias's lap, his tongue down her throat, his hands all over her body.

Susan looked around and saw that the two were not the only ones who went for each other so shamelessly. In this tent, all the rules of decency seemed to have dissolved into pleasure. Sip by sip. Nevertheless, that queasy feeling in her stomach did not want to go away.

Andi and Fanny prompted her to drink again.

Susan tried to stay in a good mood and drank.

After all, this was the time of her life.

A moment to enjoy …

She couldn't finish the fourth mug because she suddenly felt sick. Susan got up, wavering, and looked around for her friend, but Clara was gone. So was Matthias. Only spilled beer remained on the bench.

Where's Clara? Susan had to hold on to the table so she wouldn't fall. The world had gone off its hinges and lost all contours. Music, laughter, and voices around her merged into an indefinable rumble that hurt her ears.

I have to find Clara!

Suddenly, a gush of vomit flew up her throat and shot into her mouth. Susan bent forward and spat on the floor. It wasn't much, but her stomach didn't seem to be done yet.

"Clara?" She tried to look around. Her girlfriend couldn't be far, right? But it was almost impossible to spot her in this rolling, wobbling, bawling crowd.

Andi and Fanny had come around the table and held her by the elbows. Susan didn't like that very much. Suddenly she felt like she was in a vice.

"Let me go," she whispered. "I have to look for Clara."

But the siblings didn't let her go.

"It's okay. Your friend is okay," Fanny whispered, but Susan didn't believe her. If only she weren't so dizzy and sick.

She tried to squirm out of their grip when Andi grabbed her so tightly that it hurt. Susan froze. Andi's mouth was a grim line, his eyes looked cold.

"It hurts! Stop it!"

Andi didn't respond.

"You come with us," Fanny said. Her German accent was so strong that Susan could hardly understand her.

"We'll have a party!" Andi said cheerfully.

Susan tried to think. To think *clearly*! Not a chance ...

What was she supposed to do? Scream for help? She didn't even know where Matthias had taken Clara, and if that had happened voluntarily ...

She looked around frantically. But this ocean of bobbing dirndls and swaying lederhosen offered no ray of hope. They were all drunk and busy with their

21

own affairs. No one would react to her or understand her.

Maybe one of the waitresses.

Susan screamed when she saw one.

The woman had a sweaty face and carried an armful of jugs.

"Hey! Help!" Susan hollered.

The woman didn't notice her.

Or did she?

She stopped and looked over at them as Susan swayed like a buoy in the mass of drunks.

Andi held Susan's arm in a painful grip.

Black circles danced in front of Susan's eyes. "Help! I need help!"

The waitress looked at her and nodded. "*I kim glei!*" *What?*

Susan closed her mouth. Something in her was giving in. It was pointless.

The waitress fought her way through the crowd. *What did she say?*

The amused facial expressions of Andi and Fanny didn't promise anything good.

"Come with us. We go to Clara. It's okay," Fanny said.

Susan wanted to turn away. She wanted to scream and run away, but the dizziness was too strong. She had to vomit again. Andi and Fanny held her. It didn't make much sense to resist. She had to find Clara. Without Clara, she was lost. When Susan finally gave up and allowed herself to be led, Andi's grip didn't hurt anymore.

They left the tent without getting any skeptical glances. Susan was only one of many who had underestimated the Bavarian beer. An American tourist who couldn't get enough and had to live with the consequences now. In her drunkenness she looked panic-stricken and desperate, but didn't they all?

***

They did not draw attention when they crossed the overcrowded area. Susan was just one of many drunks on this early evening who staggered through the throng, supported by friends, and who had to stop over and over again to puke their souls out in front of everyone.

Her consciousness was as wavering as her walk.

Her thoughts revolved around Clara.

She had to find her.

Everything would be fine as soon as she did.

At some point people became fewer, and they were on a street Susan didn't know. Nothing here looked familiar. She would have found the hostel where she and Clara stayed only by using Google Maps, but now she didn't need Google. She had Andi and Fanny.

They seemed to walk for half an eternity until they finally stopped in front of a dark green off-road vehicle. Matthias stood smoking in front of the open driver's door, and Clara was sitting on the backseat.

Susan's heart jumped. *Thank God!*

When Fanny opened the door, Susan saw that her friend was unconscious. Her head hung down and

23

saliva dripped from her chin into the wide neckline of her dirndl.

"Get in!" Fanny vigorously prompted her by giving a hard push in her back.

Without thinking, Susan climbed into the car and sat down next to her girlfriend. The vomit on Clara's lap emitted a sour stench, causing Susan's stomach to rebel again. She gagged, but this time she held it back.

Matthias pressed himself next to her and put a hand on her knee. Fanny got in on the other side and sat next to Clara. The passenger seat remained empty.

"Everything okay?" Andi asked, who was behind the steering wheel. He had probably drunk the least.

"It's fine," Fanny replied. "Let's go."

Susan heard the words but didn't understand them. She leaned back and closed her eyes as the car began to move.

Matthias's hand lay heavy on her knee.

She knew he was just waiting to hurt her.

She only had to give him one reason. An itty-bitty one would do, she suspected.

But why?

At least Clara was here.

Probably they would take them somewhere they could rape them undisturbed and then throw them out of the car.

That would be a lesson for them.

As long as they were together, they could survive anything—and come out of it stronger. So, she allowed Matthias's hand to slide higher and higher under her skirt and finally land between her legs. His

24

fingers quickly found their way into Susan's panties, but she kept her eyes closed and pretended not to feel it.

Supplies

When curious eight-year-old Fips took a look inside the attic, he'd seen a skinny girl. She was a few years older than him, had small breasts, and hardly any body hair.

Not that Dad would have cared, back then or today. Age wasn't an issue.

Fips was seventeen now, and the girl was probably in her mid-twenties. To Dad's disappointment, her breasts had remained small, but she had gotten quite a bit of body hair. Black and dense. There was even a small dark shadow above her upper lip. Matthias sometimes complained and wanted to shave her. Dad forbade it.

He liked her that way.

And Fips?

Well, Fips refused to think about his role in all that. He had no preferences anyway but just participated and did what was demanded of him. He did it quite poorly, if one had asked his father.

After nine years, the thin girl had gradually worn out. What she'd endured—the things Fips knew about and everything he suspected in the darkest corners of his soul—haunted him in his dreams. Sometimes he imagined what it would be like to be in her place, though he actually couldn't imagine it! Not without losing his mind.

She'd been standing outside the door with her mother back then. They'd come from out of nowhere, dirty and wearing shabby clothes.

Romanians who wanted to beg or steal …

A stroke of luck for Dad, who had tortured the last girl to death just a few weeks before. He had cut her vagina so badly that she'd bled to death. After that, it had been Mama's screams that roared through the house at night, because Dad couldn't live without sex. Could you even call that sex? Mama wasn't too successful hiding her injuries, although she'd almost veiled herself like a Muslim.

Fips had been too young back then to really understand all that. All he knew was that his mom was doing better since Dad had the girl.

The monster had hidden himself, showing only his brightest and friendliest side when he asked the woman and her child into the living room for something to drink. He had poured a lot of milk and sugar into the coffee—and a portion of rat poison.

The lemonade he'd offered the girl was clean.

Soon the woman began to suffer from horrendous cramping, and Dad sent the younger children to their rooms. They were still too young to see that. Only Andi, the eldest, was allowed to stay and watch—and learn.

Mama grabbed the screaming child and shut her mouth. Dad wanted her to watch her mother die a miserable death. After all, there was no better lesson.

Fips, whom his brother had told about it, sometimes wondered why Dad hadn't kept the woman alive. Had she been too old for him? Too ugly?

Would it have mattered to Dad? His own wife wouldn't have won any beauty contest either. Fips suspected he'd probably killed her because there were two of them: One for now and one for later. Just like little children did with their candy: one part devoured immediately, the rest saved for later.

For bad times.

The woman spasmed, her cramps intensifying, puking blood and foam and squirming across the floor like a dying beetle. Andi said it had felt like an eternity until she finally died. At the end, she'd been shitting herself. Andi had described this stench well. Fips could clearly imagine it.

The skinny girl had been calm in the end. Dad had ripped her clothes off, thrown her on the floor, and raped her next to her mother's corpse. And he had enjoyed having an audience.

Fips would have instantly ripped his eyes out of his head if he had witnessed it, because these images would have eaten their way into his brain forever ... her screams, the blood ... and the eyes, which at first were horrified but in the end had been so dull that they looked dusty. Even in his imagination it was horrible.

Then Dad brought the skinny girl upstairs. Sixteen-year-old Andi had to stay and help Mama with the corpse.

That was nine years ago. Nine fucking years!

Meanwhile, the thin girl with the dusty eyes was abused by all the male members of the Koller family.

***

After sex, Fips turned away from her. Just like he always did. Dad had said it would be the last time. Andi and the others were already looking for new supplies.

That's what Dad called it.

Supplies.

It had taken Fips longer than his brothers to penetrate her for the first time, although she spread her legs very obediently and did everything she could to make it feel good for him. When his father took him upstairs for the first time on his sixteenth birthday, he just couldn't do it. Only weeks later did Dad's many lessons serve their purpose.

Sixteen, as Matthias had been—or Andi, when he was deflowered by a girl who hadn't been around for a long time—was, in Dad's opinion, just the right age to become a man.

Fips couldn't find any real pleasure in it. If you could disregard the bad smell, it might perhaps be quite nice.

But Fips knew nothing about that.

He could not disregard anything.

Never.

He only did what he had to do to at least be part of it, so that Mama would love him—if this feeling existed for her at all. And so that his siblings would respect him. So that Dad looked at him …

Fips knew it wasn't sufficient. He hadn't done enough to earn his place in this family.

Dad wanted the skinny girl to die.

He'd had enough of her.

Her belly was distended again ...

This wasn't the first time this had happened since she'd come here. Mama and Fanny took care of the births and the subsequent *disposals*. Fips had never seen one of the babies.

The girl who was chained to the floor followed him with her dusty look as he slowly went to the stairs. Dirty and naked, she lay in her own filth. Mama and Fanny regularly changed the straw on which she vegetated like a piece of livestock.

Once a day she was given the bucket.

Every now and then, if Dad allowed it, they sprayed her clean with the hose.

It was strictly forbidden to talk to her or touch her other than sexually. Fips had done it in the beginning and had learned quickly that you weren't too old for the potato cellar at sixteen.

And it hadn't lost any of its horror!

Dad had shown him how to punish the skinny girl with the whip or burning cigarettes and had asked him if he had any ideas of his own.

Not until today ...

Matthias was often up here. Apparently, he had many ideas.

If the girl had screamed in the past, they had stuffed her mouth with pig shit—or with her own. That's why she hadn't screamed for a long time. She hadn't even given the slightest peep during birth.

Could you really escape that?

Didn't someone scream automatically when the pain became too strong?

How many times had Fips asked himself such questions? He didn't know exactly what Dad was going to do, but there wouldn't be a skinny girl any more afterward. That much was certain. She would end up as a pot roast and pig feed.

Just like the others.

The idea triggered a piercing nausea in him.

He hated those pigs! He had avoided them as a child. Fortunately, the women were responsible for them. Dad had clear rules regarding the distribution of tasks. The men followed their pleasure, and the women did the dirty work. It was that simple.

The banquets were the worst.

Although Fips never noticed his mother going to the butcher or a pig being slaughtered, there was always plenty of meat in the freezer. On holidays, Mama prepared lots of it, and Dad insisted on empty plates regardless of how full they had been or how small the stomach of an eight-year-old was. Fips hated the sweetish aroma of this meat, which tasted so different from the schnitzels they had on normal days.

Dad's facial expression when chewing was different than usual. Blissful and evil at the same time. Those who didn't want to eat were beaten on the back of their heads until they forced the spongy pieces of meat into their mouths. Once Fips had actually vomited on his plate … and had been forced to empty it. Dad had made sure. Wastage was out of the question.

Fips had been reluctant to eat Mama's feast only once. The potato cellar had purified him.

Nowadays he could eat without thinking.

And not only that …

The guilty conscience he'd had when cumming inside the girl remained, but in the beginning it had been stronger.

Fips had learned to disregard the unbearable, otherwise he never would have survived his family. He would have long-since landed in his mother's pot and in the pig trough.

After he left the attic, he went into the bathroom and took a shower. He scrubbed his genitals until they were burning like fire, not wanting to smell or feel the girl anymore. He was almost a bit happy that she would soon be gone.

Too many bad memories …

Dad sat in the kitchen smoking a cigar when Fips came downstairs. Mama stood at the stove and stirred in a pot. The others would be back soon.

If things went well.

"Sit down," Dad ordered.

Fips nodded and obeyed.

"Fanny called. Everything went fine."

Fips swallowed. The air was filled with the smell of the stew that Mama was preparing. He would have puked rather than just tasting a spoonful of it, but later he would eat. They all would.

"They even have two." Dad sounded excited, his voice cracking.

Fips noticed the familiar glow in his eyes.

Supplies.

Fresh meat.

The skinny girl's time was up.

Would she be grateful?

"*You* should do it," Dad continued. He blew the smoke out of his nostrils. When Fips was still a kid, he had always found it funny.

"It's time."

Fips gasped for air. The smell of the food attacked him like a hostile invasion. The air was too thick!

Dad nodded thoughtfully. Behind his full gray beard the facial muscles were working. "Can you do that?"

Fips couldn't answer. His tongue was stuck to his palate, and he was eight years old again. What would happen if he refused? The potato cellar? Or worse? He was almost grown up and was no longer afraid of the darkness or crawling bugs. But was that really true? He still imagined himself sitting down there. Small and naked. Trembling and freezing. At the mercy of Dad.

A year ago it had felt the same. Why should it be any different now?

"I'll go with you. Okay?"

Fips looked at his mother who had turned her back to them and kept stirring in her pot. Hadn't she been listening? Why did she pretend that it was none of her business?

"What about Matthias?" Finally Fips had found his voice again. "He'll be pissed. He wanted to ..."

"It's not about your brother, it's about you," Dad rumbled.

Fips twitched. He was close to tears. Hadn't he done everything he was able to? Why couldn't that finally stop? Why couldn't Dad leave him alone?

"I know you don't enjoy fucking her. So we have to find something else for you. Don't you think so, Fipsi?"

"It's fun for me, Dad," Fips shouted. "Honestly!"

Dad laughed—deep from the throat and mean as the devil.

"Maybe you'd like to cut her or burn her. What is it, my son? What turns you on? Do you want to beat her? Kick her? Do you want to cut her tits off?"

He laughed again. "It's your choice. Take your pick."

What was wrong with Mama? Why didn't she turn around? Did she really want to do that to him? After all, she was the only one who could change Dad's mind sometimes. Why didn't she try? She certainly knew how sensitive her youngest son was!

"Dad, I ..."

At that moment the door opened, and Mitzi came in. Fips stared at his eighteen-year-old sister as if she were his last rescue. Of course, Mitzi wouldn't be any help. Fips loved her, but she was just like the others. She would never understand why he didn't want to hurt the skinny girl. Probably she would have done it herself if Dad had allowed her to.

"What's up?" She put her backpack in the corner and sniffed greedily. "Yummy, stew!"

Mama Koller turned around and gave her daughter a faint smile before turning back to the stove. Fips was ignored—just like Mitzi, who leaped across the room smiling and sat on Dad's lap.

How could she love him?

How did they all manage to be one happy family? All of them, except for Fips. He loved his sisters and mom as much as possible. For his brothers and daddy he only felt hate most of the time. So how did Mitzi manage to love and cuddle this evil gray-bearded man like that? How did she manage to be happy in this family? And why didn't Fips succeed? He had grown up with it just like the others.

"Your siblings have provided supplies. Two," Dad said.

Mitzi clapped her hands.

What did she like about it? Or had she just learned to appreciate it?

"Finally, we can get rid of the one up there."

Mitzi nodded as if it were the most natural thing in the world. A world that Fips didn't understand. He never had.

"Fips is supposed to take care of it, but he's scared shitless again."

Mitzi kissed Dad on the bearded cheek. "May I, Dad?"

What had gotten into her!

"That's men's work," Dad muttered. He smiled. Mitzi often made him smile.

"What about it, Fips? I'd like to have this done before dinner." He gently pushed Mitzi from his lap and
stood up.

He stepped next to Mama and opened a drawer. "I
definitely feel like cutting today." He pulled out one
of the knives Mama used to chop the pig feed.

Fips felt like his guts were just slipping downward.
His chest was suddenly much too tight.

Dad didn't care. He patted him on the shoulder as
he passed by, the cigar dangling from the corner of his
mouth. "Come on."

"May I join you?" Mitzi sounded pleading, ex-
pectant.

Why didn't she see the evil? Why didn't she understand how wrong it all was?

"Some other time," Dad replied.

And this time Fips knew why: Dad wanted to be
alone with him.

***

They had to turn on the floodlight because it was already dusk. At the beginning of October, the days became shorter again. Fips was already frightened of the
winter when it would be pitch dark at five p.m. He
hated the darkness. That's where the bad things happened.

The skinny girl lay on her undignified bed with her
eyes closed. She had covered her body with straw. Up
here the insulation was poor and the nights were cold.

Fips's shivering had nothing to do with the cold.

36

Without hesitation, Dad went to the girl and kicked her against her shins until she opened her eyes with a moan.

The rusty chain on her ankle jingled.

Fips had to remember that she had been up here for years. Here she had grown from a girl to a woman. Here she had been abused and desecrated. Here she had become a mother. Again and again. Did she long for salvation and the end of all torments? Or was she still clinging to life?

Dad kicked her a few more times. Then he bent down and stubbed out the cigar on her pregnant belly. She didn't make a sound. Only her legs twitched. Dad pushed the straw away, and Fips saw fresh urine seep out of her. He shuddered, but the sight seemed to get Dad really going. He opened his pants and took out his erect penis.

The girl knew what to do.

She immediately got on her knees and opened her mouth.

Fips wanted to look the other way, but he knew he wasn't allowed to. So he watched the thin girl satisfy his father orally until he moaned loudly and his loins were jerking.

Fips heard her swallow.

A sound he would never forget.

The knife almost slipped out of his sweaty hand when he realized again that it was there. Dad just stuffed his penis back into his pants. The girl lay down again

"Your turn!"

Fips hesitantly approached the maltreated body.

The corners of her mouth were white from Dad's sperm.

But he didn't have to kiss her. He didn't even have to touch her. He only had to …

The throat!

That was the solution!

He only had to slit her throat.

That would be quick. Good for her and good for him.

Fips squatted and raised the knife. He trembled so much that he could hardly hold it.

The girl stared at him; she didn't move.

"Close your eyes," he whispered.

She did so.

A pig grunted in the background. Or was that Dad's laughter?

Fips wanted to close his eyes too. Of course, that wasn't possible.

Suddenly he realized that none of them knew the girl's name. After all these years.

They had never asked her.

And now it didn't matter anymore.

Or did it?

He pressed the blade against her throat.

As if for protection she had put her hands on her belly. How far was her pregnancy? Seventh month perhaps.

Was it his baby?

No one would ever know.

"What's your name?"

Dad would not like the question. Why bother?

The girl kept her eyes closed and held her belly tight—and remained silent. She didn't want to give it to him. It belonged to her. The only thing she had kept all these years. Except for Fips, nobody had ever been interested.

He pressed harder and saw blood.

The girl flinched.

Now harder and once crosswise.

Fips knew how to do that.

He had slaughtered pigs. And rabbits.

They were hung on their hind legs to bleed out.

The skinny girl's blood soaked the straw. Now it just bubbled out of her, and she made gurgling noises. So after all, she was only a human being, too. Of flesh and blood.

Blood that ran over her breasts and her thick belly. It covered all the wounds and scars and made her body perfect again.

A perfect red.

Fips just had to look. It was fascinating. While dying, she opened her eyes widely and looked at him. Was that gratitude? Or hatred? What was the difference? Would he ever know?

Fips had completely forgotten that Dad was here when his father suddenly tapped him on the shoulder.

He turned around.

"Get up, boy! You're full of blood!"

Fips held his hands in front of his face. It was true. The blood was not only on the knife.

He would have to shower again.

Well …

"Are you all right?" Dad sounded insecure. Or was he angry?

Fips had done what he wanted. Dad should be proud of him. Finally. He got up to tell him exactly this, but his knees were like jelly and gave out under his body. Fips landed between the girl's spread legs. It was all wet and slimy there. He tried to lift himself up to get on his feet somehow—but couldn't make it.

What's the matter with me? Why can't I do that?

Fips tried again and again, but everything under him was so slick that he kept slipping … and finally landed in the darkness.

***

When Fips woke up, he was lying in his bed. How was that possible? And Fanny was with him. Fanny, his favorite sister. Where did she come from? Hadn't she been out with the others to—

Yes, of course.

Dad had gotten tired of the skinny girl. He'd needed supplies.

Fanny wore a dress and had pinned up her hair.

She was so beautiful.

Fips knew, of course, that the dress was actually a dirndl she had worn at the Oktoberfest. Thousands of people from all over the world came there to get drunk. There was hardly any better place to …

At least Dad had said so, although he had certainly not been there for twenty years. Why should he? He had his kids to take care of everything.

"How are you, little one?"

It was nice to hear Fanny's voice. She dabbed his forehead with a cool, damp cloth. That felt good.

"I killed her," Fips whispered, waiting for tears. There were none. Maybe he had finally used them all up.

Fanny nodded. "Dad is happy."

"So, I don't have to go to the potato cellar this time?"

She smiled. "Not this time."

Fips tried to smile, but it hurt his face. Maybe because it wasn't right.

"Can you get up yet? Do you want to come downstairs?" A strand of hair had loosened from her hairdo. Fanny pushed it behind her ear.

She was so pretty. A girl like her should go out with friends and meet boys. Instead, she always came home immediately after work at the hair salon and maintained only superficial contacts. Like they all did. Dad had shown them how to do it.

"What's downstairs?"

But Fips knew. Of course, he did.

"Dad's inaugurating the new girls. They're Americans. Very cute."

"Why two?"

Fanny answered with a shrug.

Fips thought, *One for now and one for later.*

They looked at each other.

Fips would have done anything for his sister. She meant the world to him.

"I'd rather lie here a little longer."

Fanny nodded. She leaned forward and kissed him gently on the corner of his mouth. "Okay. I gotta help Mama."

And, good God, Fips knew what she had to do.

***

When Clara Bricks regained consciousness, she sat slumped on the backseat of a car that rattled heavily. She smelled puke and grimaced when she realized she had vomited on her own lap. She carefully straightened herself and caught a quick glimpse through the window.

She saw trees. Only trees. And even more trees. There was nothing else to see. It was getting dark. She moaned quietly and held one hand in front of her mouth when sour gastric acid shot up. The beer! Why had she drank so much of it? Wasn't that what her mother had always warned her about? *Never drink so much that you no longer know what you're doing or where you are!*

Clara was a bad daughter. She had not listened to her mother. Susan was with her, and Clara had always felt safe with her. Too safe.

Clara pressed her lips together and swallowed the sour broth. Her stomach was like a sailboat on stormy waves, tipping back and forth, slipping too far up and back down again. She had felt like this when she'd been sitting on the boat swing with Susan before they went into the damn tent and met these horrible people who clearly weren't up to anything good.

Clara never thought another girl could be dangerous. Strange men, of course—everyone knew about that—and girls always had to be on alert. Too many men were fake and liars and did everything to get into their pants.

But they'd had this girl with them!

This pretty young woman with the great hairdo. Their sister, allegedly. What guy would go on a rape tour with his own sister? Clara never would have believed something like this was possible. What woman would do that? Absolutely not one who seemed as likeable and nice as Fanny. But it had happened.

Fanny sat to her right with her face turned toward the window. She was lost in thoughts that Clara would rather not know about.

To her left sat Susan, stiff and straight. With her eyes closed, she was forcing herself to endure the hands that wandered over her body and under her skirt.

Clara opened her mouth, almost saying something. But what would she say? The man who grabbed her friend sneered. Clara had forgotten his name, but she remembered how his hands had felt on *her* body. She hadn't just allowed it to happen somehow, like Susan did now, but she had liked it! She'd been stupid and drunk.

But the drunkenness wore off and tasted like the bitterest pill Clara had ever swallowed. She would regret that until the end of her life.

Stupid, stupid, stupid! How can you be so stupid?

She wanted to slap herself for that. She really deserved the puking, but she didn't deserve the rest, did she? She hadn't been that bad! And neither was Susan—the very least of all! They were good people who didn't harm anyone. It couldn't end like this! It should have been the most beautiful time of their lives!

They jolted through the forest for a while, on a road that was probably not intended for the public. Maybe a private or forest road. Clara was thinking about all the wicked fairy tales from her childhood. At night, her father had always read to her from this big book that had a red velvet cover, and she had never dared to tell him these bedtime stories scared her. After all, it had been the only time of the day that had belonged only to Dad and her, and she would have rather cut off an ear than admit that she didn't like the stories he told with such fervor.

Afterward, there was always a hug and a kiss. What little girl wouldn't have accepted a creepy story for that? But they weren't real horror stories, only the Brothers Grimm's fairy tales, with which Clara's dad had grown up himself.

And most of them happened in the woods.

Little Red Riding Hood.

The Wolf and the Seven Goats.

Brother and Sister.

Hansel and Gretel.

Stories from a dark time with little hope, but with happy endings nonetheless. *Happy ending* meant everyone got what they deserved ...

Susan and Clara were in the forest, and everything seemed gloomy and hopeless.

But what did they deserve?

Was this their punishment for too much thoughtlessness? Did they have to atone for wearing dirndls that were much too tight, for drinking too much beer? Wasn't it a sin to let strange men grope you? What would their parents say? Their friends?

We didn't mean any harm! We just wanted to have fun!

Clara looked down at the puke on her dress. Fun was no excuse, she knew that. There was never an excuse for a switched-off brain, as her dad always said. Maybe he'd wanted to teach her life lessons by reading her all these fairy tales. Clara had not understood the messages, but now that she was lost in the forest herself, the answers seemed within reach. She still couldn't put her finger on it, though. Her dad had wanted to warn her—not only of the big bad wolf but of the whole big bad world. Whoever ventured out there had to be strong and courageous and was never allowed to switch off the brain! Not for any beer or party in the world! Certainly not for a young man with flashing eyes!

Clara and Susan were definitely partly to blame for the dilemma they'd gotten into. This wouldn't have happened if they'd been more careful.

Diffused lights appeared in the windshield, and Clara finally saw a big house in the middle of this gloomy nowhere. Again, she thought of one of those damned fairy tales: *Hansel and Gretel.* Only in that case it had been a small hut made of tasty candy that hid the horror inside. This house looked just as ugly and unfriendly from the outside as it would be behind the door. Clara was sure of that.

The car stopped, and for a moment she considered resisting.

Susan got out of the car without looking at her. The man with the flashing eyes, whom Clara had considered to be an exciting adventure for a short time, roughly dragged her friend behind him. They had already disappeared inside the house.

The young woman, Fanny, pushed Clara out of the car. The other man was already there—Clara couldn't remember his name, but she knew Susan had let him kiss her—and he grabbed her by the arm. Clara tried to meet his gaze, but he avoided her. She felt as if he didn't enjoy the whole thing as much as his siblings did, but could that help her? As long as he stuck with them, it made no difference.

She allowed herself to be led to the door and concentrated on her churning stomach. She tried not to think about what might wait for her inside.

***

Even though the light was on, it was dark in the house. It smelled like a slaughterhouse. Clara found herself in a spacious hallway. A steep wooden staircase led to an impenetrable blackness on the first floor, but her kidnapper directed her the other way through a half open door into a large, old-fashioned kitchen where the stench was much worse.

A little woman with a crooked back stood at the stove and worked on a cooking pot that was encrusted on the outside with leftover food. Clara's stomach tried to go crazy again, so she swallowed back a bitter gush of bile.

She heard a sob and looked to her left, where Susan was undressing under the austere gaze of a teenage girl. The girl had something in her hand that looked like a long black whip, and red welts were visible on Susan's breasts. Clara tried to make eye contact with her girlfriend, but she only looked down as she stripped off one garment after another and threw them on the floor.

At a large bulky dining table sat the young man with the flashing eyes and an older bearded man, who had a small mug in front of him.

Clara felt the hand of the nasty bitch who betrayed her on her shoulder.

"Clothes away!" Her pronunciation was even worse than her grammar, but of course Clara knew what she wanted.

She hesitated long enough to catch a slap on the back of her head from the brother with whom Susan had snogged at the Oktoberfest. "Do it!"

The woman at the stove turned around and stared at her. She had a rutted face and sad eyes. Did she feel sorry for Susan and Clara?

Clara took off the dirndl. At least she got rid of the dirty puke-covered apron. She wore red underwear, which she'd put on after showering that morning. After taking off her bra, her heavy breasts slumped downward like the udders of a cow. Clara hated that. She had always envied her friend Susan for her small firm breasts, which stood upright at all times.

Fanny hit her on the plump back, and she took off her panties, shoes, and socks. The wooden planks under her feet were cold, rough, and sticky. Clara wanted to hide her breasts with her hands but refrained from doing so when Fanny slapped her again. This time on her ass. Clara was well padded, so it didn't hurt. Her ass cheeks wiggled, and she was instinctively ashamed. She stood there, frozen, waiting for what would happen next.

Behind her she heard the whip crack, followed by Susan's scream. She felt a cool rough hand gliding over her thighs from behind. She was pressed against a hard body that smelled slightly rancid, and suddenly his hands were everywhere. Clara first felt the scratchy beard on her shoulder and immediately afterward a finger, demandingly drilling itself between her buttocks and finally into her anus. She stiffened when the other hand glided over her stomach. The finger in her bottom was removed, but she was grabbed between her legs so brutally that she screamed.

Susan yelled somewhere in the background. The whip cracked. Clara didn't want to look. Her gaze was fixed on the skinny woman with the sad eyes, who responded to it without any emotion. Was that her husband, the father of these siblings?

Now he pushed Clara to the floor. She had to lie on her back, and he spread her legs by pushing his boot between them. Clara whimpered, pressing her legs together again. Then he kicked her in the stomach. Clara gasped, trying to turn around and crawl away, but somebody held her tight. She didn't know who it was. She only had eyes on the older man. He took off his trousers and took out a big dirty penis. Clara screamed and fought but couldn't get away because she was being held. It was already splashing on her stomach, in her face, her hair. She threw her head back and forth as urine splashed through the air, and she screamed.

The man stopped pissing and massaged his cock.

The woman from the kitchen appeared in Clara's field of vision. She held something that looked like a knitting needle.

The man let go of his half-erect penis and bent over to hold Clara's legs. She fought back with all her strength but had no chance against the three men. The sad woman grabbed one of her breasts and pierced the needle through the nipple. Now she no longer looked sad but somehow cheerful. Happy.

Clara screamed and panted as the guy with the flashing eyes drove a hook through the hole in her nipple. He made strange grunting noises. When he pulled at the hook, it felt like he was tearing off Clara's breast. The more she fought, the harder he pulled.

When this time the elder one spread her legs, Clara remained calm. The younger one held the hook and pulled on it as soon as she made a sound.

Clara lay still and clenched her teeth. The old man crawled between her legs. She felt a sharp drilling pain as he penetrated her. It briefly got better and then even worse as he retreated and thrust into her all the more brutally. He did so until he climaxed, spastically twitching.

Clara felt a wetness between her legs that could have been anything. She didn't want to think about it. Instead, the last really nice date with her ex-boyfriend came to mind. They had spent an unforgettable afternoon on the beach. That day Clara had felt 100 percent wanted and loved. She couldn't remember ever being so very much at peace with herself before. On that afternoon she not only loved her boyfriend but herself with all her heart. If she concentrated, she could still feel it all: the warm sun on her skin, the gentle wind, Toby's breath, his kisses, the tender touches, the tingling between her legs …

Clara didn't feel the slimy semen seeping out of her and running over her sore inner thighs. She didn't feel the rough chapped hands with the much too long fingernails. She felt no more pain or humiliation.

And when she was turned around so that the brothers could take her from behind, she didn't feel it either.

She was no longer here.

***

Two hours later Fips picked himself up and sneaked downstairs. He was only halfway there when he heard the sobbing. It had started all over again. He became so giddy that he had to hold on to the banister. Hopefully they were at least adults. He didn't know if he could bring himself to assault a child.

Dad didn't have any problems with that. There seemed to be nothing to deter this cruel man. No taboos.

His legs were like rubber when Fips teetered on. He knew they were expecting him. In this house, there were no excuses for missing a family dinner.

When Fips had been sick as a child, he still had to stuff himself with tasteless pieces of meat. And if he threw up, it had been on him to clean up the mess.

Strangely enough, he couldn't remember seeing any of his siblings ever being sick at the dinner table. Not even Mitzi. Were the others always healthy, or had Dad allowed them to stay in bed? It frightened Fips not to know and caused a suffocating feeling of unreality.

Unfortunately, time never stopped, so he reached the foot of the stairs faster than he liked.

The kitchen door was open.

As always.

Mama and Fanny stood at the counter, cutting meat. It smelled of onions and fresh blood.

Fips swallowed heavily when the girls' gaze hit him. They were sitting on the bloodstained floor. Naked. In chains. Their hair was tangled, and their eyes were panic-stricken and begging because they saw Fips and were hoping for something he could never give them.

Fips knew exactly how they felt.

He knew this terrible gnawing feeling of glimmering hope that would be shattered at any moment. Because he hadn't come to help them. He would only mistreat and rape them. Just as Dad and his brothers had already done.

Fips saw the blood on their inner thighs and the hematomas on their sore skin. And that wasn't all. The torments of these women had only just begun. Snot and tears stained their swollen faces. One had a bloody nose. Both were pretty. One was long and slender with small pointed breasts, on which Dad had apparently already nibbled. The other was stocky, with strong legs and some fat stores on the stomach and hips and large, round breasts.

Someone had driven a snap hook through one of her nipples. It was still bleeding. The other girl had a similar hook in her labia.

That's why they had screamed like that. Fips had tried to convince himself that he was only dreaming, but nightmares were a reality in this house. He would like to scream and turn away from here. That's what he'd wanted since he could think.

But where was he supposed to go? Without his family, he was nothing. They had told him that often enough. Just like those two crying women, he couldn't escape.

Soon their tears will have dried up. That was the only thing Fips knew for sure. He had seen it on the skinny girl. In the end, not even her own death could draw a tear from her. It was a long time way until these two were so far gone. Until then, many tears, much blood, and other bodily fluids would flow.

When Fips entered the kitchen, the maltreated bodies moved. Chains jingled and hooks wiggled.

Suddenly there was a sharp scream.

Only now did Fips notice his sister Mitzi sitting on a chair with her legs spread, beating the slender girl's back with a black whip. Fips knew the item. Matthias had ordered it from an online sex shop. In Mitzi's hands it looked as misplaced as a cock ring on the pope's cock.

"Not move!" Mitzi shouted.

She seemed cheerful. Shiny eyes and red cheeks.

The women paused and stared at Fips.

The whip cracked again. "Look down!"

Mitzi had some problems with the English language. Mostly she had F grades, but now she was giving commands in this language, which they followed. The triumph was visible on her face.

Fips thought Mitzi would probably beat her to death if Dad would allow it.

Mama turned around. Her apron was bloody—just like the piece of meat in her hand. At her feet stood four buckets containing slimy guts and an indefinable bloody mush. The pigs would be happy.

Fips's stomach tried to revolt, but he fought it.

"You're okay, Fips?"

"Yes, Mama. Where's Dad and the others?"

"Cleaning themselves for dinner. You missed the whole beginning." Her gaze wandered briefly over the naked women.

"The hooks were Matthias's idea." She shrugged and smiled. "The men had to hold them, and I did some preliminary work with a darning needle, but then the hooks went through pretty well."

Fips looked at the bleeding wounds again. Did these words really come from his own mother while his sisters pretended to be preparing themselves for a normal family meal?

He knew from whom the meat on the counter and the innards in the buckets had come. Nevertheless, he would eat later. Just as always.

"I'm exhausted, Mama. I'd like to …"

"You'll feel better after dinner." It was rare for Mama to talk so much at once. The *initiation* of the new women seemed to have breathed new vital energy into her—at least temporarily. Probably because Dad would then spare her from her marital duties.

Fips turned his back on the violated women. He just wanted to sit down and take a deep breath. But not here!

Then Fanny turned around and came toward him. She wore a bloody apron, but her familiar face calmed him down. Fips let her lead him to a chair.

Now the women didn't stare at him anymore. They had probably understood that no help was to be expected from him.

Mitzi grinned and played with the whip.

Why can't I be like her? Fips asked himself desperately. *I just want to be part of the family and feel like the others!*

But he couldn't, no matter how hard he tried. He wasn't one of them. No matter how often he raped and murdered, he would remain an outsider, a tolerated guest. He would never really belong.

"You wanna drink something?"

Fips nodded weakly. He thought of a cocktail of blood and bodily fluids, but Fanny only brought him a glass of water that pampered his sore throat.

Not everything was bad about this family. There was love and care—if one deserved it.

The bound women at his feet looked as if they could use a sip, but Fips hadn't forgotten the potato cellar. He would never be too old for that. And he would always be afraid.

While he was still drinking, Fanny returned to the work surface.

"Mitzi?"

"Yes, Mama?"

"Could you take the feed outside, please?"

Mitzi made an annoyed face. She let the whip snap on the table so that the poor women flinched. Annoyed like a bitchy teenager who was supposed to put her cell phone away. Mitzi didn't even have one. Her interests were different.

She rose grumpily but didn't talk back when she grabbed two of the buckets. Objections were not tolerated in this house.

Fips's right hand twitched over the whip as he stared at the women's naked asses. One tiny, the other large and plump. This one was surely soft.

He knew what was expected of him. After all, he was the only man who had not yet laid a hand on the new women. Dad would expect him to beat them up at least once before dinner.

Finally, he took the whip and stood up.

Fanny turned around and winked at him.

She would be proud of him.

Just like Dad.

He had to concentrate on that and swallow everything else.

Just like these women would swallow their own blood when he was done with them.

Hell Is Real!

Susan's eyes were so sticky that she could hardly blink. She reached out one hand and touched something cool and damp.

Clara?

She wanted to say her friend's name, scream it out and roar until her lungs were burning, but only a faint moan came out of her mouth.

Again, she blinked. She barely made out the contours of coarse and bloody wooden planks—and Clara's naked, crouched body. Blood-smeared, like her own. The cool and damp was Clara's arm. Susan clung to it with her tied hands. She wouldn't let go of her friend. At least she would try.

When the pale boy, who had seemed so harmless, began to hit her, Susan passed out at some point. The pain was overwhelming. The horror was too much. She felt her skin burst and warm blood seep out. Clara had tried to protect her face with her tied hands. But her cheeks were ripped open and her lips burst open, just like her forehead and her hands. The louder she screamed, the harder he struck. Blood splattered through the air. Susan didn't know whether it was Clara's or her own.

The boy continued until Clara was quiet and no longer moving. Only then did he focus on Susan. She tried not to scream or move. She thought that perhaps he would stop. But he went on until she was about to faint and then pulled down his pants and spread Susan's legs.

She was already so numb from the previous abuse that she felt almost nothing. The boy came quickly. He left Clara alone. She'd had enough.

When it was over, Susan rushed toward the black hole that had opened in her consciousness. She only wanted to fall and fall … into the blackness, into this darkness that tasted like lead, for anything was better than this terrible room with the wooden floor and these monsters who acted as if they were a family. Everything was better than the cracking of the whip and the force of the throbbing penises that had penetrated Susan so quickly one after the other that she had forgotten which had been the first.

She hadn't known before how that felt. She had never gone all the way with her last boyfriend because she hadn't been sure if he was the right one. Now she regretted that she hadn't, because it would have been better than having her first time with this inhuman monster. Shortly before she lost consciousness, the thought occurred to her that she would never experience what it feels like to make love. For the rest of her life she would only associate this act with fear and pain.

It probably didn't matter. The rest of her life would take place here in this horror house anyway, as far away from home as one could possibly be.

Further than the Milky Way and the whole universe.

Further than death.

***

After Fips finished with the girls, he felt nauseated, and his body trembled. His wet penis felt like a foreign object. He put it back in his pants and wiped his hands on it. He was bloodstained from head to toe.

Mama hadn't turned around once in all that time. She was busy preparing the food.

Mitzi had come in to get the rest of the buckets. Fips didn't know if she'd watched him. Fanny had sat there and observed him. Her proud facial expression drove a hot sting into Fips's overexcited tummy. The presence of his sister aroused him somehow. His erection had rarely been as stable as right now.

"You should go and wash yourself," Fanny said.

That was all she had to say? Didn't she know that Fips had done it only for her? Not for Dad or his brothers. Not for Mama or Mitzi or for himself. Only for her. His Fanny. She was happy when he managed to be one of them. And that was what Fips wanted. He wanted it for her.

"The others will be back soon," Fanny added. Her tone was not as easy to read as her expression. Suddenly, Fips wished she hadn't taken off the dirndl. In jeans, T-shirt, and the bloody apron, she reminded him a bit too much of Mama, who had never been as pretty.

"Okay," he said. "I'll wash up quickly in the basement."

The bathroom was occupied. Dad loved to take a bath after work was done.

***

An hour later the family sat at the table together.

The meat was delicious. Mama's dumplings were legendary, her gravy simply fantastic.

The naked, bleeding women were still lying on the floor. An appetizer for Dad, in whose crotch a suspicious bulge appeared. Matthias also seemed ready for the next round while he noisily gnawed off a few bones. Andi, on the other hand, only had eyes for the food.

"That's yummy, Mama, really. Once again you've topped yourself."

That was music to her ears. Mama grinned like a schoolgirl.

Mitzi chewed on some beans. She was on a diet. Fanny ate with a healthy appetite, as always, and her curves thanked her for it.

Fips had to admit the food tasted great. There hadn't been a gram of fat on the skinny girl. The meat on his plate could no longer easily be associated with the young woman he had killed a few hours earlier. You didn't have to think about it—or about the fact that she had been pregnant.

As soon as the inauguration ceremony was over, the two new ones would take their place in the attic. By then Dad would have broken them so there wouldn't be any unnecessary screaming. From then on they would only be allowed to come downstairs on select occasions. Fips didn't want to think about their bellies becoming rotund sooner or later. The thinner one was already moving again. Such a tough bitch.

Fips washed down his food with a hearty sip of beer. These women would soon be terribly thirsty, but Dad would wait at least until tomorrow before pissing in their mouths for the first time. They didn't have very much more to expect. They would get food once or twice a week. Especially kitchen waste and rotten food. Unless, of course, Dad wanted the thicker one to stay in her current shape. Then perhaps he would fatten her up.

Fips knew from Andi that Dad had done this to a girl once before. She had been instilled daily with a thick mixture of mush, milk, and honey and was severely punished if she vomited. At some point she had gotten so fat that Dad was disgusted by her. Ready for being slaughtered. Mama's freezer had burst at the seams in the following months.

Fips was very small then. He had no memories of the fat girl. But Andi remembered her. He didn't seem able to forget and talked about her to this day. Later, Fips learned she'd been a classmate of his big brother.

Dad really had the balls back then. Pretty careless and stupid, but he got away with it.

The cops had never knocked on their door.

Maybe if there hadn't been the pigs. These damn critters devoured everything that wasn't nailed down: innards and bones, even skulls, if you did a little preliminary work. Those monsters! When Fips was younger, he sometimes imagined they would grin at him. Damn man-eaters! They would probably attack you if they got the chance. Not that it would ever come to that. The pig corral was 100 percent escape-proof. Mama had taken care of that.

Sometimes she would talk to the animals as if they were humans. Fips had heard it, and so had Fanny. With the pigs, Mama wasn't as taciturn as her children knew her. When she was with the damn pigs, she sometimes laughed loudly or hummed melodies that nobody knew. Mama was herself with the pigs. Fanny said so.

Fips wondered when he was ever himself. At the family dinners? At the raping of helpless girls? During killing? In the potato cellar?

No …

Fips was almost never himself.

Only sometimes, with Fanny.

His sister not only brought forth the worst in him, but also the best. Only she could ignite the heat inside him. How did she feel? Fips thought about that whenever he stuck his penis into Dad's whimpering victims. He wondered if Fanny would feel like them, even though he knew how wrong that was. Of course! She was his sister. Of the same flesh and blood. Matthias would say that they had crawled out of the same hole. As harsh as it sounded, it was true. Fanny was his sister. Just like Mitzi. And would he have ever thought of such a thing with Mitzi? No! Good God! But Fanny was something special. Fips loved her more than his life. He did it all for her. All the cruelties. Not for Dad. Only for Fanny. Only for her, Fips tried to be part of it.

That's why he was still here and put a good face on the matter at school. They hated him there, spat at him, beat him, and despised him. Soon it would be over. Then he would go to work like Fanny and his brothers. Everyone agreed working was better than school.

In vocational school he would have to suffer further, but that wouldn't be so bad. Fips would assemble and repair machines. He wouldn't think so much about home when he had something to do. And he wouldn't be at home so often once he had a full-time job.

All he had to do was find one. He didn't have much time. He already had to repeat a class. This school year was definitely his last. Completing secondary school at seventeen was anything but a brilliant achievement, but if you came from the Koller family, it was better than nothing. Dad and Mama had never finished school. Just like Andi. Matthias and Fanny had been almost eighteen when they finished school. Who cared? Now Andi and Matthias worked as laborers on the construction site and Fanny in the hair salon. She was really good at it and had many regular customers.

Fips wanted to do something with machines. This had been his wish even as a child. He loved to get to the bottom of things and disassemble stuff to see how it worked. There was nothing more satisfying than understanding the meaning behind the big picture. To look behind the façade and finally see what was wrong …

Some objects Fips had dismantled ended up broken and couldn't be fixed. Dad's radio, for example. He had received a good beating for that. Or Andi's old TV. Andi would have loved to kill little Fips. Meanwhile, he had become more skillful, and sometimes Fips wished people were a bit more like things. Then they could be opened and repaired as soon as they no longer functioned properly.

If you were skillful, you could fix almost anything with a little calm and patience and a clear mind. But anyone who wanted to open up a living being and poke around in it to make up for something was not in his right mind and was simply crazy. Fips had learned that early in life.

Back then it was a sick guinea pig. Fanny had been so sad, and he'd only wanted to help. Shortly before, he'd gotten a watch working again after meticulously disassembling and assembling it. The guinea pig could be put back together ... but it didn't work after that. The little animal was broken after eight-year-old Fips had rearranged its intestines.

He'd never forget Fanny crying. Fips hadn't been able to comfort her. She had been cold and stiff when he'd tried to hug her.

The dead guinea pig had been lying on his desk, its limbs spread, and it was no longer breathing. He had sewn its tummy together so neatly that only a delicate white seam could be seen. It had looked like new—as long as one didn't notice the large bloodstain. It could be wiped away. Just like the little slimy heap Fips had forgotten about on his desk. Its guts. Or something like that.

At least now he knew what guinea pigs looked like on the inside. Fanny hadn't been interested. Several days had passed before she would talk to him again. She hadn't wanted to see the guinea pig anymore. Fips had buried it in the garden and had felt nothing but a dull emptiness.

He'd gained one more insight: if something lived, it wasn't made better by opening it and manipulating its innards. Beings were not like things. They broke more easily and then could rarely be saved. Therefore, he reasoned, machines were much better than living beings. They remained true to you and didn't make you feel sad. And best of all, if they didn't work the way they should, you could pry them open and fix them.

Fips sometimes wished he could surround himself with lifeless things to protect his poor heart. But he was part of a family and had responsibilities, whether he wanted them or not. It would have been easier if he had loved his sister less, but who could ever choose if or who he loved?

The advantage was that anyone you didn't love could easily be considered an object, like the skinny girl Fips had seen suffering all these years without having any considerable sensation. When someone like that was gone in the end, it hurt a little at most. As if your bike had broken down. Something was missing and you got really annoyed, but your heart remained well. And as for the skinny girl, Fips didn't even miss her.

Actually, he was glad she wasn't around anymore.

Fortunately, Mama could cook so well and they had the pigs, so nothing would remain of the skinny girl, a vague memory at most that would soon fade away.

Now they had new girls, and you had to speak English around them because otherwise they didn't understand a word. That distracted them from everything else. At least a little.

**

It had been the last weekend of the Wiesn when they had taken them to their home. A few weeks later they lay in chains in the attic, and it was almost as if they had always been there. The skinny girl was forgotten. Having two was somehow more exciting. Even Fips felt it like that, even though he'd claimed that he detested these deeds and only went along with them because he didn't know what else to do. He belonged to the family, after all, and had no other idea.

Sometimes Dad was up there for several hours.

Andi and Matthias mostly went upstairs after work. Fanny or Mitzi brought them food, usually moldy loaves of bread or soured cream, fruit with bad spots, or sausages that were a bit squidgy.

At first, the girls refused to eat. After a while, they really craved food, the way they did Dad's piss. He kept them alive with it, and Fips could only guess what kind of feelings this power trip caused in Dad.

After the first month the thin one had become bony and the thicker one slender. Their skin had taken on an unhealthy color, and they had pustules around their mouths.

Dad had allowed Mama to bring them blankets so they wouldn't get sick. He liked it when they were in bad condition, but it wasn't supposed to become too bad. When people got sick, they could quickly break.

Fips didn't climb up to the attic very often. He couldn't get used to the smell of their unwashed bodies.

Dad liked it that way, and his brothers seldom complained, but Fips sometimes took Fanny's deodorant or perfume up with him and sprayed it on the girls before he sexually assaulted them. He had done it that way with the skinny girl.

They were only allowed to be washed or hosed down, maybe once a month, with Dad's permission. It hadn't happened yet. Gradually, the skin of the young women looked dirty and the stench that came from between their legs reminded him of dead fish that had been rotting for days in the blazing sun. Moreover, they had bad breath.

Sometimes Fips dreamed of kissing a girl. He had never done that before. The women he was allowed to amuse himself with stank too much, and Dad didn't allow chewing gum or candies.

Fips thought maybe everything would change if he could just kiss the girls. They would realize he wasn't a monster like Dad and his brothers. Maybe they would even start to like him.

He couldn't really imagine what it would be like to be liked by a girl. Fanny liked him, and she was the most important thing in the world to Fips. Nevertheless, she was his sister. Only his sister. That they liked each other was somehow normal and predetermined, even if Fips felt less close to his other siblings.

He wasn't sure whether he would have been really sad if something had happened to Mitzi, Matthias, or Andi. But Fanny? He didn't want to think about that! It would break his damn heart. Monster or not.

Maybe monsters had hearts too. It just looked different and wasn't in the same spot as with normal people … Dad, Andi, and Matthias's heart was between their legs. Same for Fips …

Anyway, it would have been nice to meet a girl who really liked him. Not like those at home who were only afraid of him or at school, who avoided him when they weren't busy mocking him. Life wasn't easy for a member of the Koller family.

Fips didn't know how his siblings coped with the outside world. They'd had similar problems at school, except Matthias had mostly been left alone because of his brutality and reputation as a thug. Fips knew Andi had often been beaten up. Fanny didn't have a single friend. Mitzi was considered an outsider and was ignored most of the time.

And Fips … He had a friend once in grade school. But this boy had betrayed him, and since then, Fips was alone and fought only for himself.

Dad said they didn't need any friends. Friends were dangerous. The Kollers preferred to stay on their own. But he had Mama. Not that that would have been enough for him.

Dad lived off the girls in the attic, like a vampire. The weaker they became, the stronger he grew.

Fips would probably never understand what it actually meant for Dad to keep these women captive or why Mama never tried to stop him. Being with a girl who really liked him would be great. A girl who was obedient and loyal, but not out of fear but for love. Dad didn't seem to care much about that, but for Fips it would be everything.

To find someone who loved you the way you were.

Along with all the monsters.

Didn't the others long for it? This couldn't really be enough! Fips tried to put himself in the position of his eldest sister. Fanny was twenty-three, a pretty young woman, sweet and charming. She surely had already been in love and had been eager for a man's arms, his smell—and his cock. But she stayed here and participated in all this. Maybe she did it out of love, maybe out of obsession and madness. The boys had sex, at least, and they could live out their urges, but Fanny … she had to have desires—and dreams. Surely, she sometimes saw men on the street whom she liked.

Why do you think about others so much, Fips? What about you and your longings? What about your urges? Would you rather fuck Fanny or have a girlfriend? Everything would be so much easier if everything stayed behind these four walls. Dad knows that, which is why he rarely leaves the house. You know it. All you have to do is let go and surrender to it all. You only have to let the monster off the leash. Everything could be so blissfully simple …

He would have loved to go to Fanny and just ask her. They could have talked for hours while hiding in her bed, under the blanket. Just like they used to. Fanny had always been his anchor. A safe haven in every storm. She might not have been better than the others, but he wasn't either. The world was just awful, and they had to live with that. It hadn't given them more than this family. And didn't they say you should honor your family?

Fips thought about it as he sat on the bus on the way home from school after another exhausting day. He'd had a history test and hadn't known much. Later he sat in chewing gum that someone had stuck to his chair. Intentionally, of course. At least the others had had something to laugh about on this dreary autumn day.

Now he sat here, looking out the window and watching the gray landscape. He tried to imagine his classmates' lives, kids who just thought he was a freak. There was at least one of that kind in every class. No big deal.

When his classmates went home, there was surely a warm meal waiting. Others would enjoy some kind of snack or a frozen pizza. They probably sat in front of the TV—or more likely—with YouTube on the smartphone. They would be annoyed and unwilling to do their homework but preferred to go out and meet friends, smoking, laughing, and jabbering stupid stuff. The cell phone was always at the ready. To be young and believe it would stay that way forever. Everyone knows they will grow up and die sometime, but nobody under the age of thirty really believes it.

Nobody but Fips.

Because he knows death personally.

Because he is a monster.

How would they react if they knew about the women in the attic? Or if they knew that he was no longer a virgin and not the wimp they thought he was? He certainly had more experience than most of them. Would they believe it? Would it be the end of an innocence Fips had been denied since his earliest childhood?

The gray autumn landscape had no answer.

Fips had no idea if he had ever looked forward to going home. Maybe in the past.

He was hungry and could get a hot meal if he wanted one. Sweet meat that could have been anything, not necessarily a sad, skinny girl he had killed with his own hands.

In the place he called home, there was only madness. To distract himself and feel better after the long school day, he could go upstairs and rape two women. Or just fuck one and let the other blow him. He was allowed to beat them. Just not too hard.

Sometimes it felt really good because you could forget everything else. For example all the humiliations his classmates did to him. If they knew …!

Sometimes Fips felt really strong when he went up to the attic, but that soon subsided because this strength was not real and not deserved.

Did his siblings feel the same way? He could never have talked to them about that. Not even with Fanny. How did she compensate for all that? From time to time she watched the rapes or gave out a few blows, but otherwise? She fed the pigs and cooked with Mama.

And what about Mitzi? She was much bitchier and more demanding than Fanny. Would this really be enough for her in the long run? Won't she want a life of her own? Dad had them all firmly under his control, despite external influences. Yet they all did his bidding. They all went out and exposed themselves to these influences yet returned again and again to the insanity of the Koller house. How much longer? How long until the first one would break out?

And who would be first? Fips? Or would it go on like this forever?

Fips thought, *If you don't want this, you can put an end to it.*

But that would likely be his end as well.

And how did Fips really feel when he imagined never again going to an attic when anger or despair raged in him? No more helpless women at his mercy. No fast, brutal sex that made his insides feel so empty, like the closeout sale of a store going bankrupt. First, he would have to find a woman who wanted to sleep with him, but he knew it wouldn't be the same.

So, what would he rather do without? This imaginary girl who might kiss him voluntarily one day, or the temptation that was always there under the roof?

Fips talked himself into not having much fun having sex and just doing it so the others didn't get suspicious, but was that really true? Would he still get an erection? The feeling was already good. It was sex, and he was a man.

His classmates needed the internet and sex tapes to satisfy their cravings. Fips just had to climb up to the attic. There they lay in their chains, stark naked and ready to do anything he demanded. The idea alone would have excited most of the boys.

Of course it wasn't right. And violence was not the solution. Blah, blah, blah. Who wouldn't have done it in his place? If it was so easy and Dad was supportive?

Who wouldn't have seized this opportunity?

Two young women from the United States that no one would ever look for here.

You just had to dig out your broken English and say crazy things like, "On your knees," or "In your mouth." You squeezed their tits until they were blue or pulled on the snap hooks until they bled. Fips only hurt them a little.

They often looked really bad. Most of the time he felt sorry for them. Especially Matthias was anything but squeamish. Then he drilled his fingers into existing wounds or got a blowjob from swollen mouths.

It didn't matter to Fips. He was one of many, but the one who wasn't to blame. The youngest who only participated because his dad demanded it. He wasn't a monster, only a man! Everyone would do this, right? He couldn't help the girls anyway.

And everyone would do that in his position.

Everyone!

Susan opened her eyes. It hurt.

Everything hurt.

She licked her dry lips and moaned. She was so thirsty. When the old man took out his ugly thing, she opened her mouth like a hungry birdie. It was disgusting. Sometimes she didn't know what she was more disgusted by: herself or those monsters in human form.

She had tried to talk to Clara about it, wanted to know if her friend felt the same way. Wondered how she was holding up. But Clara hadn't spoken since they were here. At first Susan thought it was an after effect of the shock and she waited for it to get better, but it didn't. Clara often cried and sometimes mumbled something incomprehensible, but apart from that she remained silent.

Susan couldn't understand. It was so important to talk! They could have comforted each other and perhaps made a plan. They could certainly have hatched *something*. There had to be a way out of this nightmare!

Surely, they were long-since regarded as missing and were being frantically searched for. During the trip they kept in regular contact with their families, who knew that they'd been in Munich before they disappeared. Nobody knew anything about their visit to the Oktoberfest, but it didn't matter, right? The police would put two and two together.

The cops weren't stupid! Susan was sure that sooner or later they would find some trace of the girls. Somebody must have seen something. There had been so many people. Somebody always saw something! The police would search. Two young American girls wearing dirndls must have attracted somebody's attention!

And knowing her and Clara's parents, they would get on the next plane and fly to Germany. It was likely they were already here, perhaps even nearby. They would put pressure on the authorities and not leave before knowing where their daughters were.

Susan thought of her father, with his thick mustache and the vehement way he never backed down. And her mother—she cried easily and had a strong imagination. It hurt to imagine her terror over her missing daughter. The poor woman would probably collapse and need a sedative. She probably suspected the girls were being held in the basement of some madman, being tortured and desecrated—the kind of scenario you found on every crime drama on TV—and that's exactly how it was. Only it wasn't a basement.

Except there was more than one madman in this house. The whole damn clan was insane! Even this girl who was younger than Susan, and the boy who had *seemed* so harmless.

The abuse and rape weren't even the worst. After a while you even got used to it. Somehow. You didn't really feel it anymore. Everything between Susan's legs had been numb for a long time now, and she only noticed blows when they were really violent or when somebody was playing around with the hook in her labia. One of the brothers—Matthias—had once hung a string on it and led her around like a dog on a leash. Sometimes they pulled so tightly on the hook that Susan thought it would tear her labia. Somehow it withstood, and somehow Susan also withstood, although she should have broken long ago.

Just like Clara.

Something inside Clara had broken during the torture in the kitchen.

Susan had foreseen it from the beginning, now she knew it for sure. When every member of the family got their turn and introduced themselves, a few pipes had burst somewhere deep inside Clara. Getting your turn and introducing yourself—that was what the father had called it. Susan had not understood him properly, but it had been enough to comprehend what awaited her.

Later, she had tried to make some contact with Clara. First only with touches, and then, when they were finally alone, with words. But Clara had not reacted to anything. Susan suspected that she was in shock and that things might get better. But the next day—the first in the attic—Clara lay there motionless, staring vapidly, as if in a stupor. Susan had talked incessantly to her friend, at first quietly and calmly, but later she had yelled and slapped her in the face. At that moment she didn't care that someone might hear her and punish her.

The punishment had come, albeit later.

Moreover, the beatings and humiliation were nothing compared to Clara's eerie mental absence. How could Susan manage without her friend? She thought she'd go crazy if Clara didn't finally talk to her. But she hadn't said a single word. That wasn't just a shock, but a real trauma. Susan wondered if Clara had lost her mind.

Was that possible?

Perhaps she had only sent her mind to someplace beautiful and safe, where she didn't have to feel the horrors of reality. Maybe Clara was on a trip around the world again, sightseeing in Rome or Paris. Maybe she was sipping an espresso in a pretty little café or was on the Eiffel Tower looking at Paris from above. Maybe she was cruising through London on a double-decker bus. Maybe she was back home already, in her room, where everything looked and smelled as it should. Not like here. Maybe Clara was just smarter than Susan. After all, there was no reason to voluntarily stay in a place like this.

Perhaps Clara had found the salvation for eternity. A nice, warm place that belonged only to her and where she was certainly not as alone as Susan in the cold attic. She surely felt no cold or pain and knew nothing of the festering hook in her nipple. She had done everything right.

Something inside Susan screamed. *She's left me! She just walked away!* She stared desperately into Clara's expressionless face.

It was astonishing that Clara, despite her apparent absence, still responded to the orders of her tormentors. She got on her knees, opened her mouth, spread her legs—whatever was demanded of her. She drank

77

and ate as soon as she was given something, but unlike Susan, she probably couldn't taste any of it. Lucky girl. At first Susan was just angry, but now she envied Clara, who had somehow found the back door.

Why didn't she take me with her? She could have taken me with her!

So why not follow her?

Susan paused. Yeah, why didn't she follow Clara? Anyplace was better than this one. But she would stay where Clara was, no? There wouldn't be a way back. If her mind left, she would never know if there was an opportunity to escape. She had to keep her sanity. Puppets had no will and couldn't save themselves, could only lie there waiting for someone to come and destroy them. Did Susan really want that? She thought about it for days, nights, and weeks.

Now and then these monsters came and did painful things to her. Blood and seminal fluid encrusted her inner thighs. The sharp taste of urine filled her mouth, but she had to drink it to stay strong. And she had to eat. No matter how disgusting it tasted.

Recently, one of the brothers—Matthias—turned the defenseless Clara around, lubricated her with Vaseline, and penetrated her ass. Susan hadn't had her turn yet, but she knew it was only a matter of time. She was horrified when she saw the blood and excrement on Clara's butt cheeks.

If Clara had been mentally present, she would certainly have screamed her throat out. But she was in her safe place, where everything was as it should be, so that one felt comfortable.

Susan still couldn't bring herself to follow her friend, despite her envy. The reason was the crazy hope for rescue. At some point they had to find them! Mom and Dad wouldn't leave any stone unturned. Just like Clara's parents. They wouldn't give up. All she had to do was hang on, stay strong, and hold on to her mind so that it wouldn't slip away like had happened to Clara.

Because it was possible Clara would never return. At a certain point you couldn't decide anymore. Clara could die without even knowing it. It was that simple. That could be a comfort, even if it was creepy.

Susan didn't want to end up like this. She was too attached to life, and to her mind. She preferred to endure the pain.

Suddenly the door opened. This squeaking haunted her in her dreams now. Susan sent a quick prayer to heaven—*Please, not the old one! Please, not the brutal one!*—which was actually answered.

It was the youngest brother. Susan thought he was about sixteen or seventeen. The face was young and naive, the forehead full of pimples. He was lanky, and his movements seemed erratic. In fact, he seemed unsure whether he wanted to be here and do all these things.

"Hi," he greeted her shyly.

Susan knew by now how deceptive this shyness could be. After all, the boy had certainly not brought the pliers in his hand coincidentally. He had come to hurt her.

Susan straightened up on her shabby bed and wrapped the torn blanket tightly around her body.

The boy wore jeans and a hoodie with a few holes in it. His ridiculous hairstyle was probably not the only thing he was teased for at school. A strange smile played around his lips.

He pointed at the blanket. "Away!"

Of course, Susan knew what he meant, as bad as his grammar and pronunciation were. She glanced at Clara, who lay there motionless and breathed flatly. However, the boy seemed to have no interest in her catatonic friend. He never did.

Susan dropped the blanket and waited until he finished sending greedy glances over her exposed body.

"Open!"

He was talking about her legs.

Susan spread them.

He licked his lips and suddenly panted.

"Touch!"

Susan knew he wanted her to masturbate or at least pretend to. Apparently, he needed the sight to get going. She started to please herself and felt nothing but the pain of her maltreated abused labia.

He grinned, one hand in his pants. He must have had a bad day at school. One of many. And now he was here to vent.

It didn't take him long.

Susan closed her eyes. Soon she felt his familiar weight, heard the hectic breath, the well-known moaning sounds, smelled his shampoo. At least he was clean. In contrast to her.

He was young and came quickly. With the old man it often took a long time, and in the end, it was a dry and painful screw. Susan preferred it the way the boy did it. It was faster and it hurt less. He also smelled better than his father.

When he was finished, he rose and hastily pulled up his pants.

Susan opened her eyes. Their glances met.

She hadn't forgotten about the pliers he'd put on the floor during the rape.

Neither had he.

"Don't hurt me," she whispered. "Please. Don't."

He winked, the pliers already in his hand. Did he understand her? Did he even care what she said?

He had often hurt her, usually by ripping open existing wounds. He'd never brought an instrument of torture with him. Susan didn't want to think about what he could do with this thing. But suddenly the pliers disappeared into his pants pocket. His gaze was hard to read.

Susan wanted to give a sigh of relief but didn't dare. In her crotch she felt the sticky consistency of his sperm.

"I like kiss."

Why—what did he mean?

The boy crouched between Susan's legs, leaned on her thighs, puckered his lips.

Of course she knew what he wanted.

She inevitably had to think about how long it had been since she'd used a toothbrush.

The boy smiled. There was a small gap between his front teeth that made him look mischievous and somehow younger. He reminded her of someone; she just couldn't think of who.

He suddenly reached into his pocket, and Susan stopped breathing. She thought he was going to take out the pliers.

Instead, he held a small package in his hand.

Susan exhaled.

It was gum.

Only chewing gum!

The boy dropped a piece into his palm and pocketed the rest of the pack. He offered the gum to Susan.

She slowly reached out and took it. The chain on her wrists allowed some leeway.

The spiciness of the gum exploded in her mouth and made her eyes water. It was good, really tasty.

Grinning, the boy bent forward. It looked so weird it almost made her laugh.

"Kiss," he whispered.

Susan closed her eyes. When their lips met, she thought of Trevor, the last boy she'd kissed voluntarily. That had been at home in America, at a party shortly before her departure. Trevor had dark hair and a mischievous grin. His mouth had tasted of alcohol and marijuana. Now Susan only tasted the gum.

The boy's tongue was slimy and twitched uncontrollably. She tried to kiss him as she had done with the other boys, alternating with her tongue and lips. At first he seemed confused, but eventually he joined in and it got better. They found a rhythm. For a moment Susan almost forgot where she was—and with whom.

She felt dizzy.

When she fell back on the hay, he stayed with her—his tongue in her mouth. She almost forgot that he'd raped her a few minutes ago, and now they were making out like teenagers. Shouldn't this have happened before sex? The world was upside down here.

Susan might have lost herself in that kiss if a hard voice hadn't suddenly penetrated her ear.

"Fips! What the hell are you doing?"

The boy let go and jumped up as if stung by an adder. Susan opened her eyes and saw the stocky old man with the potbelly and nasty little pig eyes.

She pulled her legs up and wrapped her arms around them. The gum lay in her mouth like a dead animal and still tasted spicy. She swallowed it without thinking.

Meanwhile, the boy stumbled toward his father. "Nothing, Dad. I only …"

"Did you kiss her? You know we don't kiss hookers!"

"Yes! No! I mean I fucked her. I only fucked her!"

Susan didn't understand what they were talking about because they spoke German. The old man was angry, that much was clear. And the boy was afraid. He almost wet his pants. But why?

The father let his son stand there while he came toward her. Susan wanted to shrivel up and disappear, but she couldn't go anywhere. The heavy chain on her foot was attached to a massive iron ring that was firmly embedded in the floor. On long nights of despair, she had already tested how tightly anchored it was.

She sobbed uncontrollably as the old man leaned over her. He grabbed her face and squeezed her cheeks so tightly that her mouth opened by itself. He distorted his face and shook his head in disbelief.

"What did you give her?"

"Dad, please, I only wanted to …"

"*What did you give her?*" he roared.

"Gum!"

The old man laughed. "She swallowed it. That bitch! Fucking slut!"

He noisily hawked up snot and spat the slimy lump into Susan's open mouth. Some of it landed on her upper lip, the rest …

Susan gagged. She tried to turn her head away, but the old man held her in an iron grip.

"Swallow it! You're so good at that!"

Susan didn't understand a word he was saying, but she knew what he wanted. She closed her eyes and swallowed. Then she licked her upper lip.

The old man roared with laughter. He let go of her, already fiddling with his zipper.

"The slut is hungry today. She needs another load."

Susan closed her eyes again, dreaming herself to the place where her friend Clara was.

***

When Fips followed his father downstairs, he still tasted the gum and felt the woman's tongue like a phantom in his mouth.

The kiss had been fantastic and worth any punishment. At least that's what he tried to tell himself. Besides, the girl had been punished though neither the gum nor the kiss had been her fault. Dad had beaten her half unconscious with his bare hands anyway. He was probably angry because he hadn't managed to ejaculate into her mouth. Instead, he stuffed her mouth with hay before he beat the hell out of her.

Fips was hoping she'd make it. He liked her and would never forget the kiss. It was probably his first and last one. She had tried really hard, as if she'd liked it. Fips had to hold onto this memory. He wouldn't have much more in the next few hours.

His brothers and sisters were home by now, and Dad called everyone into the kitchen.

He made Fips pull his pants and underpants down to his ankles, just like when he was a little kid.

Dad ordered him to lie face-down on the table and then whipped his ass with the buckle of his belt while everyone watched.

Fips vowed not to cry, but by the end he sobbed like a baby. When Dad was finally done and Fips was allowed to get dressed, he trembled so much that Fanny had to help him.

Without a word, Fips followed his father to the hatch of the potato cellar in the back of the house. Cold and windowless. Dark as death.

Dad used his flashlight to guide Fips's climb down and made him crouch in a corner.

Dad slammed the hatch.

Fips was alone.

His back and ass were on fire. The floor he sat on was cold and damp.

He was eight years old again.

He still could taste her. Fips would have preferred never to eat or drink anything again, just to keep that taste. For the next twenty-four hours he probably wouldn't do that anyway. He'd have to stay down here at least that long. Maybe even longer, because he wasn't a child anymore and still hadn't learned anything.

Why always him? Why couldn't he just let it be?

The idea of kissing her had been stupid and foolish. Nevertheless, he hadn't been able to stop himself. She had tasted really good. Well, it was because of his gum. But what she'd done with her tongue had been more than a normal kiss.

Fips tried to concentrate on that, ignoring the pain. Ignoring the coldness and darkness. Ignoring what might be lurking, crawling around down here and on him. Disgusting black creatures, scurrying like roaches, the living outgrowths of a nightmare.

He once again made it into the potato cellar. Would that ever get any better? Would he ever stop making Dad angry? Why did he always spoil things? The others didn't understand. Fips had seen it on their faces. They would have loved to hit him with something themselves.

"Why are you like that?" their gazes had asked. "Why can't you just stop?"

Somehow Fips really couldn't stop. Dad's rules were simple. Even a moron could have abided by them without a problem. But he couldn't do it because in his heart he didn't want to. That was probably the reason. Dad's rules were stupid and pointless. Only a dickhead would adapt to something like that without questioning it.

Only a dickhead!

And Fips didn't want to be a moron or a puppet! He didn't want to do everything his father told him. He wanted to live and have his own experiences. He wanted to love and kiss and be without fear. He didn't want to be a monster anymore. How would he ever be able to stop as long as he lived in this house? With this family?

The others did not understand him. Not even Fanny. Everything seemed obvious to them. They accepted Dad's will as if it was their own, his word being law. Was it conviction or lack of alternatives? Fips could have asked Fanny, but he didn't expect her to answer honestly. Maybe she couldn't. Surely she would have helped him if she'd known better.

He pressed his lips together and tried to hold on to the taste—and to the feeling.

Somehow it was better than sex. After all, sex was just a mechanical process, something nature had created to ensure the survival of the human race. Kissing was a real feeling. Passion. Fips had felt alive—and loved. As if she had seen a real human being in him at that moment, not just some monster who came to hurt her.

It had been worth it.

Every single second.

If he had the chance to relive that, he would happily accept another beating and spend time in the potato cellar.

Anytime!

Anytime

Helga forgot the time when she was with the pigs. It seemed to stand still out here. She watched the animals eat, sleep, or roll in the mud. Sometimes they grunted at each other, pushed others away, or even bit them. Like in any family. Sometimes it worked and sometimes it didn't. In the house, Helga was the housewife and mother. In that order. Out here she was just Helga.

The pigs wagged their tails like dogs when they were scratched behind their ears. There was nothing and nobody else that Helga had ever pampered like these critters. Her children had experienced very little love and affection. Not because she didn't want to give it, but because she didn't know how. Children were not pigs.

And Peter?

Well, he was her husband. She had sworn to honor and love him until death parted them. And she had given her best. All the time.

Peter had wanted offspring, and he'd mounted and screwed her like an animal. It looked actually more loving with the pigs.

Helga never complained. She came from difficult circumstances, had been beaten by her mother and abused by her father and a few uncles. She only knew from the pigs that sex could be something beautiful.

She was seventeen when she met Peter, an acquaintance of her father's. Just some farmer with whom her father did business. Helga was such a business. Nobody asked her what she wanted.

Peter wanted her, and her father was happy to get rid of her, so she went with the stranger, who ran a small farmstead in the forest. His family was dead, and despite his young age, he took care of the house and the farm by himself. He urgently needed a wife for the household, the cooking, and for having children. Helga was good for all that. Her father had never planned any other *purpose* for her. Just like Peter.

If she didn't obey, Peter hit her, but it happened rarely. Actually, only at the beginning in bed, when she didn't immediately understand how he wanted it. She wasn't allowed to touch him.

Her hands could just as well have been tied up during sex—just like the girls and women he held in the attic.

The first one was already there when Helga arrived. She was an ugly, middle-aged woman who was all gray and had no teeth left. Nevertheless, Peter had laid down with her more often than with his young wife.

Helga didn't know where he'd found the old hag. She never asked any questions. Never.

One day—almost three years later when Helga was pregnant with her first son—Peter dragged the woman's lifeless body into the kitchen. The body was already gray and wrinkled. Her head was literally hanging by a silken thread. He'd probably cut too deep when cutting her throat. Helga was shocked, but when Peter gave his orders, she listened well and did everything exactly as he wanted.

He showed her how to cut up the body and take out the innards, and which parts to freeze and which to give to the pigs.

After the initial disgust subsided, Helga even liked it somehow. Above all, it was fun to watch the pigs eat.

Peter was also happy with her. That meant everything to her.

A little while later he brought home a young woman who barely understood German. She was dressed like a hooker.

This time he let Helga watch.

Peter ripped off the sparse clothing from the whining woman and inaugurated her in the kitchen. Later he took her to the attic, and Helga only saw her when she brought her something to eat every few days or on holidays, when Peter let her into the kitchen where she crouched naked under the table while they ate. It was as if these women and girls were owned by the family.

Sooner or later, however, they always ended up dead on a tarpaulin in the kitchen, where Helga had to cut them up. Peter called it women's work. He had a clear idea of what women and men had to do and continued to do so with his children.

They already felt the strict hand of their father at age. They were brutally punished when they were ill-mannered, such as by not emptying their plates, giving unwanted answers, or giving Peter a wrong look. He beat the hell out of them with his belt, forced them to eat with the pigs from a trough, or locked them up in the potato cellar.

As for the chastisement of his offspring, he was as creative as with the torture of his victims, but in terms of the kids' sexual development, one could call his attitude and points of view archconservative. Before their sixteenth birthday, the children were not allowed to approach the attic. Those who did and were caught—like poor Fips—felt their father's severity in all its harshness.

Naked skin and embarrassing poses weren't good for minors. For this reason, there was neither television nor internet access in the house. The children grew up with discipline and order before Peter confronted them with the full extent of his perversions on their sixteenth birthdays, to eventually turn them into what he was.

Helga knew Peter made monsters of their children. What should she have done? She was a monster herself—unable to love her own children, but her panties got wet when she watched the copulating pigs.

She could sit for hours with a piglet on her lap, whereas she put her son back to his bed after feeding him. She let him scream for hours and generally only touched him when absolutely necessary. Somehow, she didn't like his smell. And he felt strange. Almost like the baby doll she'd played with as a child and which Uncle Willi had used to show her what he thought girls liked.

Helga couldn't stop thinking of that doll when she looked at her little son. Uncle Willi had drilled holes in it with a screwdriver. In all the places where she had holes.

Helga had hated that doll!

But she had also loved it because it was the only toy she had. Uncle Willi had destroyed it for her. And her husband destroyed her and her children.

By the time Andi was two, she had Fanny, a cute little girl Helga was unable to love any more than her son. It was even a little harder because Fanny was just like the doll Uncle Willi had defaced. Fanny was also very small when Peter first let her feel the belt. As far as that was concerned, he made no difference between the sexes.

Fanny was allowed to go to the attic for the first time on her sixteenth birthday. Her job was to help Helga take care of the prisoners and learn how to cut up a corpse. Before that, she had only ever seen the meat when Helga had processed it, but innocence ended in childhood in the Koller home. Peter wanted it that way, and no one could stop him.

In the meantime, Helga bore five children, who had grown up without her love and became monsters. She could only stop thinking about it when she was outside with the pigs. When she had to slaughter one, it hurt more than she could handle. The pain was eating its way from her heart into her body, stopping her breath and weakening her limbs. She had felt this way as a little girl whenever Uncle Willi told her to get the doll.

At some point it smelled like him.

Helga's babies smelled like that.

In comparison, the stench in the pig corral was a real treat. Shit smelled better than madness.

Helga was forty-five now. No age for a modern woman, but Helga was not modern. She just grew old and developed a crooked back.

After Fips's birth, Peter tried screwing her, but she hadn't become pregnant anymore.

He hadn't touched her for years now. Helga was okay with that. Sometimes she touched herself when she was with the pigs. At least that didn't hurt anyone. The men in her life should have followed her example.

Sometimes she got scared when she thought about the future. Would it really go on like this forever? Would Peter be able to keep the family together in the long run? After all, they weren't really a family, just a gathering of monsters.

Maybe one of the children would get sick of it someday and want a life of his own. What if he or she reported the family to the cops?

Peter said they wouldn't do that because they were part of it themselves. Helga had a different opinion. If all this was ever revealed, no one would blame the children, even if they had grown up by now, because you couldn't choose the family you were born into.

Except for their youngest, Fips, everyone seemed to get along quite well with it. But Fips stepped out of line again and again. He brought the prisoners water or other things without permission and did not hide the disgust he felt for his father and his brothers.

Helga noticed that Fips was different from the start. He never hit as hard as Peter wanted, and it took him longer than his brothers to rape his first woman. Helga was sometimes a little proud of him. Unfortunately, his rebellions had only managed to land him blows to the head and trips to the potato cellar. Nevertheless, he was a member of the Koller family. A thug, rapist, and murderer. A monster. And when he was small, Helga neglected him as much as her other children. She just didn't know how to be a mother. A baby was not a doll with holes.

It was easier with the pigs. They weren't monsters just because they ate guts and the remains of corpses. It was in their nature. They had no feelings, no complex thoughts, and no conscience.

Since yesterday, Fips was in the cellar again. Luckily it was the weekend, otherwise Helga would have had to excuse him at school. He had allegedly fed one of the girls gum and had kissed her. Clever boy—but also pretty stupid. He should have known how Peter would react to such a violation of the rules. After a good beating, he sat alone down there in the darkness, surely terrified.

Helga would have been afraid, but she couldn't help her son, even if she'd wanted to. She never would have dared talk back to Peter or do anything behind his back. She would rather kill herself—including the children and pigs.

Fips was old enough to take responsibility. He should know by now that it didn't make sense to be defiant. Despite all the rebellion, he ended up doing what his father wanted, even recently committing his first murder.

The two new women didn't speak German, and Helga wasn't sure whether it was a mistake to keep two at once, but that was Peter's decision. She would never object him. The two were probably from America, which was really damn far away. Who would find them here? As long as everyone kept their mouths shut—and they always did—it shouldn't be a problem. In the end, there would be nothing left of them anyway.

Helga leaned over the fence and stroked the head of a pig. "You'll make sure all traces disappear, won't you?"

The pig grunted in agreement. It looked happy. Helga was also happy. She felt warm. Everything would be fine.

***

Fips thought he was dreaming until he realized the loud sobbing was real and coming from him. It filled the darkness and echoed off the damp walls. He had slept last night, but he was still here. Good God. Still. Fips pressed one hand against his mouth and forced himself to stop crying.

Like he had done in the past.

It was terribly cold. His teeth rattled, making his jaw hurt. How long had he been here? He didn't know, had lost all sense of time. Down here he would be a little boy forever, no matter how much time passed. But he hadn't forgotten the kiss, even if the peppermint taste of the gum was only a memory.

What had it been like for the woman? Did she still think of it while she was trapped in her own darkness?

Did she think of him? It was crazy, but somehow Fips wished for it. He wanted to be missed and desired. He wanted to be important. To somebody.

You're important to Fanny.

Was that really true, or would she quickly forget him when he was gone? Did he really mean more to her than the others, or did he just fantasize because he couldn't bear the truth?

What is the truth?

Maybe that Fips was just a monster.

Nothing but a monster ...

What if he had to stay down here forever? If the hatch just remained locked? He would die. He would wither like a dying old tree. And nothing would remain, not even a memory, because that only worked if the person was cared for.

Fips wasn't loved enough to be remembered. Maybe he was forced to be evil so that at least that part of him would remain. You didn't always have a choice. Bad people knew that.

I just want to get out of here! Please! Please let me out, God or whoever is responsible for me! Don't let me rot down here!

Dad was responsible for him, and he wasn't here. Maybe he was in the attic or kitchen. That all seemed so far away.

Just like Fanny.

Fips hugged his sister in his thoughts and hugged himself in the cellar.

That gave him a little warmth.

But not enough.

"What's the matter, sweetie? Are you cold?"

Fanny sighed. She was freezing. Maybe she'd thought too much about Fips in the cellar.

Matthias took off his jacket and gave it to her.

"Thank you." Fanny put her brother's jacket over her shoulders. That was better.

She stared through the foggy windshield into the darkness. There wasn't much to see, just a few barren branches and the blackness of the cold night. Fanny would have loved to see a few stars, but it was too cloudy. The weather forecast had predicted rain and they were always right when they said it would rain.

Matthias lit a cigarette and winked at her through the smoke. With the three-day stubble he wore for a few months now, he seemed older and a little daring.

Fanny twitched when he shoved his hand between her legs—a twitch of delight. Fanny liked it when he touched her. She leaned back and closed her eyes, trying to relax.

Matthias's kiss tasted of cigarette smoke and cheap whiskey. They had emptied the bottle together. They knew it was risky being out here. With every warm sip it felt less dangerous. All they had to do was mind the time and not stay out longer than an hour. They also had to come home separately.

No one would think they were in the middle of the woods in Fanny's little VW Polo. Why should they? If Dad asked, Fanny would claim to have visited a colleague after work. As far as Matthias was concerned, he often wandered alone through the woods at night looking for wild boars. He had already shot boars bigger than calves. Damned bastards! They endangered the tree population and sometimes even attacked humans.

Fanny was fed up and couldn't keep track of the dates she'd had to cancel. People thought she was an uptight lesbian. She would love to go out with a man. She imagined it would be so classy and special, almost like a fairy tale. What girl didn't want to be taken out on a date in style and with class? Fanny thought of a fine restaurant, where one put cloth napkins in one's lap and drank wine from crystal glasses. She would wear a pretty dress with sequins and an artful hairdo. Unfortunately, in her everyday life, there were rarely reasons to dress up. The greedy looks of the drunks at the Oktoberfest had been a balm for Fanny's soul.

Her brother Matthias had been looking at her the same way recently. A few months ago, he had sneaked into her room one night, and Fanny held her breath as he crawled under her blanket. His stiff cock had pressed pleasantly against her thigh, and it didn't take long for Fanny to get rid of her nightgown and panties. Matthias's manner was unbridled and demanding. Fanny liked that. Real men knew what they wanted— and they took it. Fanny finally experienced her first time at age twenty-three.

Of course, losing her virginity to her twenty-year-old brother hadn't been on her agenda, but Matthias had experience and the right amount of determination. He knew exactly which buttons to press on

Fanny. The fact that he was usually assaulting defenseless women in the attic didn't bother her because it had always been that way.

Matthias could be incredibly brutal. Many times Fanny had watched him beat and rape women.

He could also be tender.

Like now. Fanny put her head back and groaned unbridled while Matthias sucked on her clitoris.

She was the only one he pleased orally. None of the women in the attic would ever get this kind of enjoyment. At least this made Fanny feel special and made her heart beat faster.

As always, the foreplay was short and sweet, the sex fast and hard. Fanny was happy with it. They didn't have much time.

Afterward, she wrapped herself in Matthias's jacket again and sucked on the cigarette, which he held to her lips.

"Everything okay?"

She nodded, but it wasn't true. Her head was much too full. She was worried about Fips down in the basement. She also wondered how the rest of the family would react if they knew about this fling.

"What do you think Dad would do if he caught us like this?"

Matthias shrugged. "He'd probably lock you in the attic. As for me ..." He grinned. "He'd shoot me like one of those damn boars."

Fanny felt goose bumps spreading on her arms and legs. "You really think so?"

Matthias shrugged again.

If he was serious, he risked a lot to be with her. That was as frightening as it was exciting.

"We're his children," she countered weakly.

"He'd never tolerate that," Matthias said. He didn't give the impression that it worried him too much.

Fanny could do nothing to stop herself from shaking.

"Hey, sweetie." Matthias put his arm around her trembling shoulders. "It's all right. Don't be afraid. He'll never know."

He smelled as good as he tasted.

"What we do is wrong," Fanny whispered.

"Have we ever done anything right?"

Fanny thought of the attic, of the potato cellar, of all the women who'd ended up on Mama's stove—and under her hatchet. The pigs had taken care of the remains.

Right? Good God!

She shook her head. "Probably not."

"It's not our fault." Matthias pressed her even harder against himself. "We never had a choice."

Fanny thought about it.

She remembered Matthias's expression when he tortured a woman. He didn't look forced, but blissful. Matthias was much more brutal than Andi and Fips. Sometimes even more brutal than Dad. Did he really have no choice? Fips at least tried to rebel against it now and then, but she had never seen Matthias do that. His brusqueness was also masculine and therefore a large part of his attractiveness to her. When he fucked her, she always had to think of how brutal he could be and how he made the other women suffer. That made her really horny. Just like now, when he pinched her nipples and demandingly licked her face.

Fanny smiled, and her brother smiled back.

Maybe they would both die if Dad ever found out, and maybe it would be worth it.

Anytime.

***

When the hatch opened, Fips first thought it was a dream and sat still. The cold had penetrated his limbs and made them stiff. Every motion was painful. But then he saw Fanny's familiar face in the semidarkness and struggled to get to his knees. Fanny reached out, and Fips clung to her hand like a drowning man. She helped him to his feet and hugged him.

Warm.

She was so warm.

Fips didn't want to cry, but he did. His legs trembled and refused to work. After three days down here without a drop of water, it was no surprise.

Fanny led him all the way to the kitchen, where Mama stood at the stove as usual and didn't even glance at him. Mitzi was also there. She grinned nastily. Fips sat at the table and greedily grabbed the bottle of water that stood there.

"Slowly," Fanny cautioned him.

Fips couldn't stop himself. He downed the cool liquid until his throat hurt and his stomach began to revolt.

Fanny took the bottle away and put one hand on his shoulder. Fips gasped for air like a fish on dry land.

Although his body wanted to get rid of the water and fought vehemently against it, he wanted to grab the bottle and keep drinking.

Fanny didn't let him. She knew better.

"Take a break or you'll puke."

She was right, but Fips didn't care. The most important thing was to drink, damn it! He was a bit angry with his sister but obeyed her.

It was better.

Fips stared at his mother's crooked back as he waited for Fanny to hand the bottle to him.

Mitzi had sat next to him and watched him like an exotic animal while she chewed on a strand of hair that was already all soaked.

"So, how's it been? You look like shit."

Sure, he did. Fips didn't pay attention to her. He looked at Fanny, who was wearing her long hair down today. Mitzi would never be so pretty.

Finally, he was allowed to continue drinking and did so until the bottle was empty.

"Mama excused you for today, but tomorrow you can go back to school."

"What day is it?"

"Monday."

Of course. On Friday he'd been locked up. There was nothing like a chilly weekend in the damp cellar. Fips was still freezing, although it was pleasantly warm in the kitchen.

"You can take a shower and lie down for a while. Later there'll be something to eat."

Mama was already working on it. Fips just didn't know if he was in the mood for that damned meat again. But he just nodded and almost started drooling when Fanny put a banana from the fruit bowl in his hand.

"So, you won't starve to death until then." She winked at him conspiratorially. But Mama was here. And Mitzi. There was no conspiracy between them, as much as Fips would have wished for it. He took the banana and forced himself not to open it until he was upstairs in his room. It was the most delicious thing he had ever eaten.

Christmas

The quiet tootling of Christmas music. The scent of fresh-baked cookies. The aroma of mulled wine. That's how Fips knew it from the old days. The house was filled with tinsel and festivities. The girls decorated the tree, and the boys set up the Christmas crib and installed the outside lights.

Christmas.

When he was small, Fips had loved that day. With time, he had succeeded in gulping down the unappetizing meat for dinner without tasting much of it. Afterward there was always a delicious dessert.

Even today, he walked around the house like an excited seven-year-old, sniffing Mama's pots and Fanny's scented candles. Mitzi hung tinsel and kitschy colorful balls, which Fanny had bought, on the tree in the living room. After the meal, the family would gather here to give each other presents. Each child received exactly one gift from their parents. It had always been that way.

When he was small, Fips had wished for remote-controlled cars or Legos. Later a cell phone or a laptop. Most of it he never got.

Nowadays there was nothing more beautiful for Dad than a naked woman wrapped in a chain of lights, whom he could assault sexually to his heart's content while his children unwrapped their presents and sipped Mama's eggnog. Christmas was an important feast for the Koller family. Dad had decided so. It was less about the gifts than the cozy get-together. There was nothing like a juicy pot roast in the company of your loved ones. Mama added dumplings and red cabbage, and Fanny made tiramisu for dessert.

Could there be anything better? The best opportunity of the year to pretend they were a normal family.

Well, at least if it hadn't been for the women in the attic. Since Fips was sixteen, Dad insisted they come down on that day. They weren't allowed to eat and spent most of their time on their knees or lying on the floor, but somehow, they were still part of it.

Dad liked when the whole family watched him abusing the women. Since Fips was old enough and none of the children had to be sent to their room anymore, he enjoyed it to the fullest when they all watched this spectacular show. They should know he was having fun.

Later it was the boys' turn. By then, Dad was usually already watching TV. He loved Christmas programs. Even commercials. It would probably always be a mystery to his kids and wife why he liked it so much. It was strange that a man like him behaved like a child on holidays and demanded the same of his family. He was like a naughty boy in a candy shop who just couldn't get enough. Regardless of the consequences.

Fips had once asked him—yes, sometimes he had the guts—how Christmas had been celebrated in his family when he was little. Dad's response had been a violent fit of rage; Dad had thrown decorations around and slapped Fips in the face. Apparently, this question hadn't conjured up any positive memories.

Why was it so important to him now?

And why did the women have to be there? Perhaps because Dad knew exactly how painful it was for them to be reminded of their own lost lives on Christmas Eve, because everyone associated Christmas with family and contemplative get-togethers. No matter what the reality. Only the illusion mattered. A game with emotions that wasn't always fair. Dad knew that.

And the others? Well, they (of course) put on a brave face, just like they'd been taught. Fips also had to admit that naked women wrapped in tinsel and sparkling Christmas lights looked pretty good and made you lust for more. It was exciting that Dad involved them so much in the ceremony. That made Christmas an adventure, although for most children it became rather boring as soon as they learned the Christ Child and Santa Claus were just illusions. For Fips and his siblings, it had only become exciting since the last of them had reached age sixteen.

Last year a woman died on Christmas because Dad had fed her glass balls until she bled to death internally. The torment included Dad, Andi, and Matthias alternately *feeding* and raping the woman with, among other things, a Christmas tree stand—and her death had taken several hours. She had been a Polish prostitute Matthias had picked up on the street and brought home especially for the feast. A *gift* for Dad that had earned him bonus points.

Fips was already sixteen then, but emotionally and physically he wasn't ready to participate. He would never forget those screams that echoed loudly throughout the house, so throaty and full of blood. The skinny girl had also been there on that evening.

The extra gift for Dad resulted in a delicious roast on Christmas Day and made not only the pigs happy.

Such gifts, however, were rare. Much too dangerous. Nowadays it was not so easy to let people disappear. You had to be on your guard at all times. This year they were lucky again. After all, there were two. One for now and one for later.

After months of torture and abuse, the two women were in poor condition. Some wounds didn't heal anymore; they had lost a few teeth and Matthias had to scrub their skin with soapy water until it was fiery red and burst in some spots.

They stood there motionless like candles when Fanny attached chains of lights, tinsel, and other decorations on them. She hung Christmas tree ornaments on the snap hooks. Clara had a red one on her nipple and Susan a golden one on her labia.

Dad liked it.

Fanny did their hair, braiding with little bells and golden threads and made up their pale faces with lots of lipstick and eye shadow.

Dad was thrilled to bits.

This time they were even allowed to sit at the table in the living room during dinner. One whined quietly because Matthias had rubbed salt and chili into her wounds. The other one looked much worse but stayed quiet. She hadn't spoken for a long time. When Dad shoved a small glass ball between her lips, she chewed and swallowed it without batting an eyelid, while trickles of blood ran from the corners of her mouth. It was scary. The other got pretty loud when Mitzi scorched her belly with a candle. Dad silenced her with duct tape because it disturbed the meal.

Fips tried to concentrate on the taste of the roast, which was pork this time. Mama looked as if she was going to vomit at any moment. She loved the stupid critters.

The gagged woman's eyes grew bigger and bigger as she watched the family eat. She'd been starving for more than a week. The other didn't seem to care because she had turned into a numb robot. Her mind had long since left her body.

Fips admired her. He would have done the same if he'd been in her place. Why suffer pointlessly like the other one?

He wondered if she remembered the kiss.

It was certainly the only halfway beautiful thing she had experienced lately. Fips smiled and winked at her, but there was no reaction. She only had eyes for the food.

If Dad was in a good mood, maybe he'd take her outside later. Pig feeding. There was nothing more amusing for him than a naked woman crouching with the pigs in the mud and fighting for a few bites out of the big trough. At this stage they had no dignity anymore and were ready for anything. Dad loved that.

He had raped the skinny girl several times directly in the pig corral because he could no longer contain himself. Of course, you had to be careful. The pigs could become quite aggressive.

Fips wondered if he would like the sight when Dad stood up for his mandatory toast.

There was a moment of devotional silence.

They even stopped chewing.

All of them.

***

Susan is still a little girl of six or seven. She sits on the porch with Dad. On his lap. Because this is the best place in the world. Dad drinks beer from an ice-cold can. Sometimes he teases her and presses the cold metal against her heated cheek.

Susan giggles and licks her ice cream. Watermelon. A summer taste.

There are many summer scents.

Susan's sunscreen.

The freshly cut lawn.

The heated grill.

Mom's lemonade.

Susan wants to stay here forever, be a little girl forever. She sees a butterfly and waves at it. Dad laughs. That sounds funny. Like marbles rolling. Susan has two in her hand. Her prettiest and most colorful glass marbles that look a bit different from each side. She will never forget how it feels.

The marbles, the ice cream, Dad's lap, this day …

As a child there is only the here and now and a shadowy idea of the future in pretty colors. You can't really imagine what it will be like to be an adult. All you know is that it will happen someday. And then it will be good. Why not? Basic confidence is stronger than all doubts.

Suddenly Susan is frightened and flinches. Someone pinched her belly. Dad?

She turns to him. Dad is no longer there.

She sits alone on the garden swing.

Where did he go?

Susan looks at her ice cream, but it's gone. Just like the lush green lawn, which all of a sudden looks disgustingly brown and burned. This is how it suddenly smells—penetratingly dead and burned.

The sausages on the grill are black. Not burned but decomposed.

That's what death smells like.

The lemonade in Mom's pitcher doesn't look much better. Dark yellow with green mold on the surface and full of indefinable particles floating in it. It must have been there for ages.

Susan rises and looks down at herself.

She is no longer a little girl but an adult woman.

That shouldn't have happened!

She turns around and wants to go through the door into the kitchen to her mom, but the door is locked, secured with a rusty chain. The whole house suddenly looks different. Old and derelict. Weeds have grown through the wooden planks on the veranda. The windows are barricaded with old boards.

Susan staggers backward. She can't believe it, can't understand it. Years have passed since she was a little girl, and now everything is old and broken. Decayed and rotten. Because in reality that is what happens when we grow up. No colorful future. Only decay and rot.

Why did that have to happen?

Hadn't she always been a good girl? Hadn't she given her best?

None of it was good enough.

Again, she feels a tweak somewhere, and Susan realizes she's naked. Wires with colored lights cover her skin. It looks like Christmas, but it doesn't feel like it. She wants to raise her hands and get rid of them somehow, but they're not free either.

Why is she tied up?

Who would do that to her?

She just wanted to sit on Dad's lap and be a little girl again.

Damn it, why doesn't that work?

***

Susan opened her eyes. Her lips were taped, and she could hardly move. Her belly hurt terribly! She sat at a festive dining table. Together with the family. This was a goddamn nightmare!

Clara was here, but she might as well have been far away or dead. Unlike Susan, she would never again leave her most beautiful place in the world. At least not in this life. Clara looked horrible. She bled from countless wounds and had—for whatever reason—bloody lips. It could have been strawberry jam. In another place, in another life, in another story. Tears ran down Clara's cheeks. But that was only her body. Clara was in a place where she didn't notice any of it.

Susan had tried to do the same, but unfortunately her most beautiful place in the world was rotten, and now she was here again to watch these monsters eat.

Why did her stomach hurt so much, and why did it smell burned? Susan noticed that the skin on her belly was reddened and partly burned. She had blisters. Who had done this to her?

At this moment one of the brothers, Matthias, bent over to Clara and shoved a small glass ball into her mouth. An ugly crunch was heard. Clara chewed, swallowed, and bled even more.

Susan moaned and turned away. She couldn't watch it any longer. What would she do if someone put a Christmas tree ball in her mouth? Spit it out. Again and again. As long as she could. She wouldn't make it that easy for these sadists. This she swore to God!

Wasn't that exactly what sadists wanted?

Susan's gaze stayed on the boy who had kissed her. Now she knew who he reminded her of! He looked a bit like her cousin Travis.

At Christmas the whole family came together. What would it be like this year? Had her parents already returned to America to move on somehow? Or were they still here and didn't give up?

They couldn't just give up! Because in reality the house with the pretty veranda wasn't old and rotten. It was still there, just like Susan. It wasn't over yet.

The family dinner of horror continued. The father shoved one forkful after another into his greasy mouth. The mother ate slowly and with a face of stone. She looked old, although she probably wasn't. The daughter, whose hairstyle Susan had admired at the Oktoberfest, wore a top with a deep neckline again today. Her chestnut brown hair fell over her shoulders in gentle waves. While eating, her gaze repeatedly wandered to the opposite side of the table, where one of her brothers sat next to Clara and fed her Christmas tree balls from a small bowl while he seemed to enjoy every bite.

Susan sat next to the teenage daughter who had burned her belly earlier and was now poking in her food as if she wasn't hungry or afraid something might be wrong with it. She was a grumpy girl with coarse features and fiery-red acne.

At the opposite end of the massive dining table, the boy who reminded Susan of her cousin sat next to the oldest brother, who had been flirting with her at the Oktoberfest. Andi wore his hair in a ponytail and looked well-groomed, even with a three-day beard. He had the best body and lasted the longest during sex.

The conversations at the table were brief and only in a whisper. Well-behaved or just completely insane? Susan suspected the latter.

Despite all the fear and pain, there was a demanding rumbling in her stomach. She felt the hunger of a lifetime, and the scents of the Christmas feast brought her senses to life. If they had given her something, Susan would have eaten. In spite of everything. She would have stuffed the meat into her mouth without even wondering for a second where it might have come from. At a certain point, nothing mattered anymore. It became all about survival.

But the meal ended without her getting a single bite. Only Clara crunched away and was still bleeding. The bowl with the balls was almost empty. Susan's friend had closed her eyes. Again and again her body twitched uncontrollably, and blood ran constantly over her chin.

The sight broke Susan's heart.

The family's plates were now empty, more or less. The younger daughter had hardly eaten anything. It wouldn't make her any prettier.

"Mitzi? Don't forget the pigs!"

The girl looked at her father with a gaze that spoke volumes, but she just nodded and rose. Susan had understood nothing, just the name of the girl who left the room through a door next to the woodstove. The gush of cold air flowing into the kitchen revealed that the door either led outside or into an unheated part of the house. Susan didn't know much about Bavarian farmhouses from the turn of the century. She only knew that if she could ever leave it, she would never voluntarily enter one again.

The old man stood up and approached her.

Susan was wrapped so tightly that she was almost unable to move. She moaned behind the tape as the man lifted her, panting.

"Will you help me, Matthias?"

Again, Susan had only understood the name. Matthias, the prettiest and most brutal of them all, grabbed her roughly under the arms. The two men carried her toward the door Mitzi had just disappeared through.

Susan would immediately find out where it led. Whether she wanted to or not.

***

After Dad and Matthias carried the woman outside—at least she would get something to eat—Mama cleared the table. Fanny and Andi helped her.

Fips sat there staring at the woman with the bloody mouth. She surely could use a glass of water, but he wouldn't give her one. Who would want to spend the holidays in the potato cellar? The chain of lights hid most of her wounds and the festering nipple with the snap hook. That made her more beautiful—a little. Fips thought she smelled like someone who didn't have much longer to live. He knew the odor well but still wasn't sure whether it came from inside or outside the body.

"Dad wants her to be clean. Can you take care of that?"

Fips looked at his brother and raised his eyebrows. Clean?

"You know. Away with all the frippery. Just skin, bones, and meat."

Meat.

Fips could have guessed. After all, there were two more holidays to come, and there wasn't much left of the piglet. They were a big, hungry family. Mama said that sometimes, if she said anything at all. A big hungry family.

Carnivores.

Monsters.

Damn cannibals!

Why did he have to do that?

Cleaning her didn't just mean that all the Christmas stuff had to be taken off. Fips had never had to do it alone. Especially not on a living object. To be on the safe side, he asked again.

"While she's still alive?"

"Yes, you idiot! That's the real fun, right?"

Clean

It was so cold in the stable that Susan felt relief for a moment when she was thrown into the pig corral. The mud, which consisted mostly of old and new shit, was quite warm. She lay on her stomach and tried to somehow fill herself up with that warmth as quickly and as well as possible. Dozens of pink, dirty bodies surrounded her. The animals grunted like crazy and tried to chase each other away from the feeding trough.

"This you chance. You eat or you death."

That was some lousy English, but Susan understood what the men wanted her to do. She was supposed to fight with the pigs for rotten kitchen waste. If she didn't get anything or if she refused, she would die.

She was hungry, that much was certain. She had already gotten a mouthful of pig shit. The stuff in the trough couldn't be worse. The pigs seemed to like it, judging by the collective smacking.

Susan got on all fours. They had freed her from the Christmas decorations using a hedge trimmer. Now she only wore handcuffs and could move quite well. The pigs that stood directly at the trough scuttered around, trying to bite other animals away.

Susan tried to push herself between the fat bodies. She heard a nasty grunt and felt a stinging pain as one of the pigs bit her shoulder. The men laughed and shouted something at her that she didn't understand. Anyway, Susan was seized with ambition. Again she pushed forward, ignored the bites, screamed, gasped, and groaned, hit the fat bodies, even grabbed a young animal and threw it aside.

Finally the trough was in sight, filled with a slimy mush that had a sweetish smell of decay. Never mind. Essentially it was food. Life. She wasn't done with it yet. And so Susan Edwards threw herself headlong into the most disgusting Christmas dinner of her life and experienced a triumph that could not be put into words—in no language of the world.

***

After the trough was empty and the pigs had calmed down, the men climbed into the enclosure. They kicked Susan in the ass with their rubber boots and raped her. But they couldn't take away her satisfaction. This pitiful woman was full of shit and robbed of all dignity, but regardless of that she was sated. For the first time in months, Susan Edwards was sated.

***

When a body had to be *cleaned*, it was usually the women's job. Mama had taught her daughters how to do that. The hair had to be shaved off for easy access to the brain. The teeth were knocked out, crushed with a hammer, and mixed with the pig feed. Eye-catching physical features such as tattoos, piercings, or birthmarks were removed or cut out.

When that happened, the women had always been dead. This one was still alive, or at least breathing.

Fips knew what to do. He had watched often enough.

But if she was still alive ...

"I ... I'm not sure, Andi," he stammered. "I've never done this before."

"That's exactly the point. Dad's afraid you're too soft. After the last action ..."

What was he talking about? The kiss? That was already weeks ago! And Fips had paid for it. He had taken his punishment like a man. So what the fuck was that? Why couldn't Dad finally let it go and take care of his own crap?

"Maybe Fanny will help you a bit," Andi said.

Mama didn't react. Once again you could only see her crooked back above the kitchen counter. She had just let in some rinsing water.

Fanny turned around and smiled. "Sure, I'll help you."

"Remember to let her live. Dad wants a little bit of fun on the holidays."

"Doesn't he already have that?" Fips could well imagine what Dad and Matthias were doing with the other one in the pigsty. They would definitely not kiss her.

Andi shrugged. "Can he ever get enough of it?"

***

It was easier with Fanny and maybe even a little bit fun. She took care of the woman's hair while Fips cut the decoration off her body. When he was done, her wounds had reopened. Dark yellow pus dripped from her nipple. This had to hurt, but the woman didn't make a sound when Fips tampered with the snap hook, part of which had grown into her flesh. Blood and pus splashed out. Fips felt as if a big hand was squeezing his stomach and turning it around again and again. He had no choice but to pull the hook out with brute force. The woman twitched and fresh tears ran, but she remained silent and didn't fight back.

When he finally got the hook out, her skull was already bald. She didn't look like a woman anymore. Fanny had first used scissors and then a razor without drawing a single drop of blood. Not yet.

The maltreated nipple looked terrible. It wasn't a sexual characteristic anymore but only a deformed piece of shredded flesh. Fips let the snap hook disappear in his pants pocket. He didn't even think about it.

Fanny scratched her head. "Who does the teeth?"

That would be bloody. Fips shuddered at the thought. "Would you do that?"

Fanny laughed. "If you prefer."

He preferred it. Absolutely!

***

When they dragged Susan back into the kitchen, Clara was gone. In her place, a bald, horribly disfigured shop window dummy hung on the chair at the dining table.

Susan screamed sharply. Her stomach started to spin and wanted to get rid of everything she had just triumphantly eaten. Suddenly it didn't matter anymore. Neither did the pain in her abdomen and the unpleasant throbbing of the countless pig bites on her skin.

"Clara!" She hardly recognized her own voice. "*CLARA!*"

Her friend didn't respond. She had closed her eyes and was breathing flatly. The dark-red blood dripping from her disfigured mouth stained her neck and chest and ran down to her belly button. And those little white things? Were those her teeth?

"Clara!" Susan couldn't help but scream her friend's name. The two men who had just abused her held her firmly and kept her from running over to Clara.

The pretty girl and the boy who looked a bit like Susan's cousin stared at her. The boy stood behind Clara and held her head with both hands. The girl was right in front of her face. She held a pair of pliers in her hand and was smeared with blood herself.

"What are you doing?" Susan yelled. "What are you doing to her?"

The girl lowered her hand with the pliers. She looked like a little child who had just been caught stealing sweets by a strict mother.

"Stop it!" Susan screamed. "Please, stop it!"

But they wouldn't stop. Neither now nor later. This nightmare would never end. The men held her. Their grip was painful and merciless.

The mother stood at the sink, showing no emotion at all, not even turning around. What was wrong with her? What was wrong with this family? How could

God allow something like this to happen? They couldn't be human beings!

Susan fought back with her hands and feet. She had never fought so hard before, not even in the pig enclosure. It was all useless. Father and son dragged her to the door and brought her up to the cold attic. From now on she would be alone here. She knew Clara wouldn't be back, and she was absolutely sure it would soon be over for Clara.

When Susan lay chained to her bed again, she wrapped herself in her ratty blanket and rolled herself up like a fetus.

She was really alone.

Clara would stay in her beautiful place until it was over. Hopefully! Susan wished she had such a place too, but hers was old, rotten, and broken, and she didn't know a better one. There was no safer place than Dad's lap and the porch of her parents' house.

Clara had been her best friend. Together they should have had the time of their lives, but it had become a time of death. Susan hoped they would meet again. Very soon. In a beautiful place.

***

The woman had freaked out when she saw her mangled friend. Fips couldn't blame her. He was also struggling with his dinner and his self-control. Only Fanny and Mitzi, who had sat at the table to watch, seemed completely relaxed. As if this poor woman didn't look like a plucked turkey. As if everything wasn't full of blood.

Mama seemed not to care. She devoted herself to washing the dishes, as if there was nothing more important in the world.

"Oh my, that was awful," Mitzi said. She sounded indifferent and bored.

"Yes." Fanny agreed with her and started working on her victim's disfigured mouth again. A few teeth were left.

Fips didn't know what to say. As soon as he tried to put himself in the place of these women, his stomach ached and his heart pounded. Why didn't Fanny and Mitzi feel that way? They should be able to understand best what was going on with these poor girls! What would it be like if someone did that to them?

At that moment, Dad and Matthias returned. They stank of pig shit, a smell that only differed insignificantly from human excrement, if at all. Again, Fips's stomach flipped.

Dad came very close to have a look at the *cleaned* girl. He even put a fecal-encrusted finger in her mouth to check her teeth.

"All torn out! Bravo!"

Fanny smiled as if she had done something special. She was proud of her father's compliment.

Fips could understand her. He would have been just as happy. Instead, he was happy for his sister and smiled while he ignored his disgust and nausea.

Dad hadn't finished his *inspection* yet. He touched the countless wounds with shit-smeared fingers and played around with the festered nipple until fresh tears ran down the woman's face. His pants bulged, and he greedily licked his lips.

Suddenly there was a rippling sound. Urine leaked out between the woman's legs and dripped to the floor. That made Dad laugh. Matthias grinned.

"No way," Dad said to Fanny. "She must lick it up."

Matthias clapped his hands. "She has to be punished!"

Will that ever stop? Fips thought desperately.

His sister had already grabbed the moribund woman by the neck and forced her to her knees, and although she caused even more mess with her bleeding mouth than she could remove, she did her best. For minutes. Until Dad finally decided it was enough. He preferred another round of sex.

***

That night Fips lay awake for a long time before he decided to get up and look after his sister, who was sleeping on the same floor two doors down.

"Fanny," he whispered at her door. "Fanny? Are you awake?" He opened the door a little. It always smelled good in here. Perfume and soap. "Fanny?"

Fips noticed a movement and the rustling of bedding. "Fips? What's the matter?"

Now he saw her. Just a shadow in her bed. The face was a blurry blob framed by dark hair.

"I can't sleep."

"Come in and close the door."

Fips didn't have to think twice.

Fanny turned on the bedside lamp and sat up in bed. The straps of her spaghetti top had slipped. She looked beautiful and sexy.

With a beating heart, Fips approached the bed. He hadn't been here at night since they were children. Was it okay to sit on the bed?

Fanny reached out. Fips grabbed her hand and let her pull him onto the mattress. His sister radiated a pleasant warmth, and her face cream made her skin shine. Fips was disappointed when she let go of his hand.

"What's wrong?" Her pure face was beautiful without makeup.

"I can't sleep. I always have to think about it."

"About what?"

"What we're doing with that woman down there. How long is she going to stay alive like this?"

Fanny shrugged. "That depends."

"Don't you feel sorry for her?"

"Do you pity her?"

Fips swallowed the lump down his throat and nodded. "Yes. Of course. She's a human being. That— that's not human!"

"She's not one of us, Fips. We have to think of ourselves, not of any strangers."

"Can you do that, Fanny? Because I can't."

"You hurt them. Are you going to say you don't enjoy this?"

Fips tried to think about it. He was a rapist, a murderer, a monster. Nevertheless, he had a conscience.

126

He was not indifferent. And when it was fun, it hurt even more afterward.

"Sometimes I enjoy it. And I'm even sorrier about that."

Fanny kept silent. Was she thinking about it, or was she just tired?

The break was too long for Fips. "Fanny?"

"I know what you mean," she finally said, to his surprise.

"You—you know?"

Fanny nodded. "It's the same with me."

"You feel sorry for them?"

"They … I … we …"

"Though you laugh at it?"

Fanny laughed quietly and dryly. "You can learn that."

Fips thought about it. She was right. Of course! You could learn to laugh.

"Mama will cut the first piece of her tomorrow," Fips whispered. "And Dad will let her live on. Do you really want to see that? Do you want to sit at the table and eat her meat while she watches you do it?"

"You know I don't," Fanny protested.

"Then you have to do something about it!"

"Why me?" She was angry and all the more beautiful. "Why did you come to me with it? You know what happens if we resist Dad! You've been in this damn dungeon often enough!"

"I came to you because you're the only one I trust. Do you understand that, Fanny? I'm not sure if you're on my side, but I know you'd never betray me."

She wouldn't. He could see it on her pretty face. She took Fips's hand and squeezed it so hard that it hurt a bit. A little was fine.

"Never," she whispered.

"I love you, Fanny. And I need you. Without you, I'd have gone crazy long ago."

She embraced him, pressed his tear-stained face to her warm chest. "I love you too, Fipsi. So much."

"What can we do? Maybe run away? Get help?"

"We must not rush things. We have to be careful."

"But ..."

"Give me some time, Fips, okay? Let me think about it. It's our family, after all."

What a word! Family. What a joke! But that included lying in the warm arms of his sister. Family. Such happiness!

***

Clara was in her beautiful place. She had already retreated there months ago. Just as soon as she was raped for the first time, during the first terrible hours in this horror house. Now they were lone fighters. Each had to do the right thing for herself. Clara's beautiful place was the day by the sea. The endless day by the sea. Warm yellow, soft blue, brilliant white, and golden brown. She had this day in her memory. She had taken it into her heart.

Even a year later she would describe this day as perfect and the best one of her life so far. On her journey with Susan there had been many more unforgettable highlights, but nothing compared to this day.

Because she had spent it with him. With Toby. Her sweetheart.

After that day at the seaside, Clara had been with Toby only a few more weeks. There had been no more perfect days. Only this one, which would remain the best forever and ever. Because it was love. Something that everyone should experience at least once in their life. Real love. The way it looked and felt. The way it tasted and smelled.

The sun was high in the sky; she noticed the deep blue water, the white sand, Toby's tanned skin. The smell of salt and sunscreen. Beads of water on Toby's muscular chest and in his flaxen hair. The perfect example of a surfer boy. And he was hers. On this one day, they were one. Perfect and complete.

Somehow Clara had actually managed to make this day last forever. Here on the beach in the soft warm sand there was no pain. No fear. Toby was here to keep all evil away. He would protect her. Forever and ever. Because here they would be a couple forever. The party where Toby kissed that other girl weeks later would never take place. The hatred that had befallen Clara and killed everything good would never come over her. Because here on the beach, under the hot American sun, there was no room for hate. No room for fear and shame or anything negative. That's why Clara had chosen it. Here she could stay and be safe forever. Everything else that had happened didn't matter. Not here.

As she caressed Toby's soft skin and played with his silky curls, she fell asleep over and over again. Warm and blissful. After all, there was nothing to be afraid of. Nobody could hurt her.

Sometimes, however, a few clouds came up, covering parts of the sun and casting creepy shadows on Toby's pretty face. Then Clara shivered and felt a ghostly twinge in her body.

The solution was simple. She jumped up and grabbed Toby's hand. Together they ran into the water. Warm, deep, and made to forget. They splashed around for a while. Until all clouds and shadows disappeared.

Clara was so grateful for this place. She hoped Susan had found a similar place. The idea of leaving her friend alone with this disgusting family made Clara's heart heavy. Even on a beautiful summer day like this. She couldn't change anything, for she wouldn't return. Never. After all, she wasn't crazy!

Toby was so sweet—maybe even a little sweeter than in reality—and making love with him was like cotton candy. Warm, soft, and cuddly. Clara would never stop. Not voluntarily. Here on the beach she felt beautiful and loved, and she had the greatest body and the whitest teeth.

Here she was the queen.

***

Clara Bricks wasn't a queen at the Kollers' house. Actually, she wasn't even human anymore. In the morning of the second Christmas day she had been tied naked to a chair and looked more like a maltreated doll. Clara had no hair, no breasts, and no teeth anymore. Would Toby have recognized her? Deep gaping wounds filled the space in her stomach and thighs and where her breasts had been— everywhere this terrible woman had cut out her flesh. A stinking puddle of vomit, blood, urine, and liquid excrement had formed under the chair. Clara's festered nipple swam in a tin bucket in a disgusting broth of blood, fat, and tissue remains.

Helga Koller was a diligent cook. She cut away everything that could be inedible or hard to digest.

The pigs would be happy.

At the sight of the dying body, Fips's eyes filled with tears. It smelled like a slaughterhouse, but Mama stood completely unimpressed at the stove as the fresh meat sizzled. He wanted to grab her by the bony shoulders to turn her around and scream into her face: "Why? Good God! Why?"

Instead, he walked on jelly legs and sat. The others were already at the table, watching him. Only Andi was missing. What was he doing? Lately he was away more often. Did he have a girlfriend? Or any other secret?

Dad will knock that out of you, Fips thought with resignation. He knew best about it.

Fanny looked very pretty today. She wore a top with sequins and a tight, obscenely short miniskirt. What did Dad think of that? Or Matthias, who stared at his sister quite overtly? Grinning. Fanny's cheeks were red, and she seemed embarrassed. Why?

Fips tried to meet her gaze, but she looked away on purpose. Was she still on his side?

Mitzi had tried to dress up fashionably. She wore a floral dress and glittery tights. Her styling attempts always looked like accidents. If she ever intended to turn men's heads, she would probably have a hard time.

Fanny had it in her blood. She even succeeded with her own brothers. Dad, on the other hand, only had eyes for the pathetic creature on the chair. One of his hands was between her legs, the other between his own. Fips did not believe there could be a more disgusting being than this man. How could they have allowed him to live out his morbid instincts so shamelessly in front of everyone? When they were children they might not have known better, but now they were grown up and weren't allowed to rely on excuses forever.

At that moment, Andi came through the door. He seemed rushed. Was something else on his face? Something that Fips felt as well? It almost looked like disgust. At least for a short moment. Andi took a seat and breathed heavily.

"Where have you been?" Matthias wanted to know.

"On a walk," Andi replied briefly.

Who believes that? Fips thought.

Matthias also seemed skeptical but didn't ask any further questions. It was much more interesting to watch Dad groping the half-dead woman.

"She can taste a piece of herself afterward," Dad said with excitement.

Fips had his doubts that the woman would still notice. If she could eat at all. He preferred not to imagine himself in her situation.

"First we have to clean up here. This makes you lose your appetite! Fanny? Mitzi?"

The sisters rose reluctantly. That was a lot of shit, piss, and blood on the floor.

"Fips can help you," Dad suggested.

Sure, who else?

Matthias grinned. Of course, he liked that. Fips would have loved to smash his clenched fist into his face. Instead, he got up to help his sisters.

They wouldn't eat until everything was clean.

So Much Luck?

Andreas Koller had walked the earth for twenty-five years and had long since realized his life was a pile of shit. As the firstborn, he had been exposed to his father's madness early and unfiltered. For a long time, he had no doubt that his dad was doing the right thing. He had reached puberty, then the magical age of sixteen, and then experienced his first times as a desecrator and rapist. Dad had set an example for him and pretended that it was the only right thing to do.

Andi's classmates lived for the next party, a pretty girlfriend, a good gradutation, and a rewarding job. Later they would have relationships and families. And what did Andi live for? Dad might have had an answer, but Dad's answers didn't interest him since he'd grown a beard.

As a child, it had been easy to believe and do everything your parents taught you. No one had prepared Andi for adulthood. It had come over him like a bomb, just as powerfully and suddenly.

Sometimes he wished his brain just hadn't developed any further. He would be a child in a man's body then. There were worse things. At least he wouldn't have to worry about his mind and his soul's salvation.

For years he'd been thinking about going to the police. Why not? Whatever he might lose wasn't worth a tear. If he had finally gotten his ass up, the last girl might have been saved. And the kidnapping of the two new ones wouldn't have happened in the first place. Instead, he had gone to the Oktoberfest and done what a good son did to make his father happy. He had packed away his pity—and his mind—at the same time.

If you didn't know any other way, it wasn't so difficult to get a hardon when looking at helpless women. Andi didn't know what it would have been like if he'd ever experienced a normal sex life. He didn't know if he would like cuddling. Maybe. Maybe not. Some things lay in the genes, after all. What should you do about it? Or could he have done something? Could he still do it?

That was the question he had asked himself again today. For two hours he had crisscrossed the forest. He knew all the hidden paths. He had wondered how lucky a man had to be to get away with such monstrosities for so long.

Of course, Dad had been careful, at least most of the time. He had carefully considered which girls or women he could grab. Best of all were those nobody would miss.

There had been only one exception.

Steffi.

How old had she been back then? Sixteen? Andi had known her since elementary school. Later they attended middle school.

Steffi had always had a few kilos too much on her ribs, so she was bullied. *"Fat Steffi!"* they shouted at her on the bus each morning. Already as a child, Steffi was pushed around during breaks and pushed into the dirt. So she preferred to stay under the canopy at the safe entrance and eat her snack there. Buttered bread and clementines. Sometimes a treat called *Milchschnitte*—a delicious candy known also as *"milk cuts."* Sometimes two. Her drinking bottle was blue with a yellow cap. Why did Andi still know that?

Fat Steffi … It had been under the canopy where they had befriended each other. Steffi gave him half of her clementine, and Andi let her taste the dried meat that Mama always wrapped for him. Steffi wore a colorful anorak and dark-green corduroy pants. Children like her were laughed at and were the last to be picked for the team for dodgeball. Children like her were a laughingstock as long as they weren't invisible. And that got even worse when they became teenagers.

Andi understood Steffi. He felt close to her because he'd also been such a bullied child and had become exactly the teenager nobody wanted to deal with. He knew he smelled strange and his clothes had been out of fashion for at least ten years. Mama had been given the clothes. She never bought anything new. And she never touched him. He had gotten used to it. Because you got used to everything. Just like the women in the attic. Dad's women. And since his sixteenth birthday, also Andi's women. Dad always said that: Andi's women. He should touch them and be as rough as possible. It was only good when it hurt and when they whined and rolled their eyes.

Sometimes Andi imagined that he would hurt the girls in school like that. Or the teachers. Or people on the street. He wasn't sure what to feel about it. It seemed clear to Dad. It aroused him, so it was a good thing for him.

Andi couldn't get an erection at first, but then he thought of Steffi and that worked. He liked her laughter and the dimples in her cheeks. It had never bothered him that she was fat. Quite the opposite. It made her softer. Andi had already felt this as a child when she was pushed on the bus and hit him with full force. Although she was heavy, he caught her. After all, he was a man. Like Dad. He was strong and could hurt anyone if he wanted to. If only he wanted …

Instead, he let himself be insulted. Then as now. Just like Steffi. He pulled his shoulders up and looked down when his classmates on the other side of the street whistled loudly and shouted vulgarities at him. Just don't listen. That was the secret. Steffi did the same. That's how they had become good friends—and a little more at some point. When Andi thought back today, it was clear to him that he had never had a boyfriend or girlfriend like Steffi again. He had liked her very much. So much. Nevertheless, he had killed her. Because it was his fault. Because he was stupid and selfish.

One day Steffi had cried at school. And this time it wasn't because of her classmates. During the break under the protective canopy—a place they had claimed for themselves when they were adolescents— she told Andi about her father and her brothers, who were probably very mean, and about her mother, who was dead. She had died during Steffi's birth, and that was why her family hated her so much. That was

137

Steffi's theory. On this cool, rainy day in spring, she didn't want to go home. Absolutely not! The evening before must have been really bad. She had a few bruises.

Today Andi wondered why they hadn't talked to a teacher back then. Steffi would probably have gone to a home or assisted living, and maybe they would never have seen each other again, but at least she would still be alive, twenty-five years old and maybe—hopefully—doing things better than her or Andi's family.

Unfortunately, things went differently. Because as a sixteen-year-old outsider, you didn't think of asking for the help of those who otherwise let you down. Andi had felt strong enough to take care of the matter himself. He wanted to hide Steffi in the small hut behind the house in the middle of the forest. There he used to play with his sister Fanny. Fanny would certainly not tell anyone if she found out about it.

At least that's what he thought.

In fact, fourteen-year-old Fanny would have done anything back then to please her dad. On the very first day, she told him about the young girl in the hut, for whom Andi had stolen food from the pantry.

Dad waited until it was dark and everyone was asleep before going out to the hut. He already had the chains with him. Steffi didn't stand a chance, and before she knew it, she found herself on a straw bed in the attic. Naked and in chains.

The next day was a Saturday, and Andi had to sit in the cellar for hours after he had gotten the beating of his life, while his father abused the sobbing Steffi. Her screams could still be heard even in the potato cellar and had been burned into Andi's brain and heart forever. God alone knew how much she had suffered. Dad liked that she was a little fatter. He pinched and bit the bulges of fat on her stomach and kneaded her round ass until it was black and blue.

On Sunday he started fattening her up.

At first Steffi fought against it. She refused to open her mouth, spat out the disgusting milk porridge, or put a finger down her throat to vomit. But Dad had his ways. After about a week she let herself be fed submissively and—in case she threw up—licked up her own vomit without being prompted.

Dad liked the variety. So far, he had only raped slender women. The disadvantage was all the dirt she made. She often had diarrhea, but Mama had to take care of that.

Dad made sure Andi saw his former classmate regularly. But to the chagrin of his father, Andi never managed to get an erection at the sight of Steffi, who was so cruelly maltreated. Nonetheless, he had to beat her and stuff the porridge into her mouth. Her imploring eyes were his punishment. He still dreamed about them.

At school, everyone was talking about the missing girl at first. They searched for her, but probably halfheartedly. Her family didn't really seem to care. The father expressed his suspicion that she had run away. For an unstable sixteen-year-old, this was quite conceivable.

Andi waited a long time for a witness who had seen Steffi get off the bus with him, but his station was the last one and no one had noticed that Steffi had stayed on the bus for so long. Not even the driver, because they had gotten in and out at the rear. Nevertheless, part of Andi waited until today for someone who had seen something. Someone who knew Andi was to blame for Steffi's disappearance. And for the nightmare her life had turned into.

It took almost two years for Dad to get tired of her. By then she had become so fat that her own mother wouldn't have recognized her, and she had lost her mind. But Andi hadn't forgotten the clementines and the milchschnitten. And he always thought of Steffi when he was alone under the canopy, while the other teenagers were smoking behind the gym or telling dirty jokes in the schoolyard. He would never be one of them. Not now and not ever. With Steffi he had lost more than just a girlfriend.

When she was dead, he ate her. As dried meat. Under the canopy. That's why she was part of him. Forever. The darkest and most disgusting secret a man can have. Something that made you lose your mind, but there was enough of Andi's left to be disgusted by the sight of the mutilated woman sitting at the table with his family on Christmas day. And he felt compassion, even if it wasn't obvious. Nevertheless, he ate straight-faced. And when Mama asked for more meat, he cut a piece about the size of a fist out of the bloody thigh. Without changing his facial expression.

Dad fed the poor girl her own body parts. At least it was fried, and Andi hoped she didn't really understand what she was eating. She couldn't chew anymore, but she choked it down somehow after Matthias had rammed the fork into her leg.

His little brother Fips looked like he was about to puke. He was weak. Andi had often wondered if he should confide in him. Although he was sure Fips would be on his side, he doubted the boy's perseverance; his rebellions had always ended in the potato cellar. If you really wanted to change something, you had to be strong and stay calm. You had to grin and bear it and you weren't allowed to chicken out under any circumstances!

Fips was older now and could perhaps be of some help. Mostly he was still a little boy with shit all over his pants. Andi wouldn't take a chance that Fips would screw up or even stab him in the back. It wasn't easy. Wait and see. That's all he could do at the moment. For Steffi, he had not been able to do more. And in the end it had been too late.

***

That night, Fips sneaked to his sister's room again. She wasn't there. Confused, he stared at the empty bed and the rumpled sheets. Maybe she was in the bathroom.

Fips left the room and looked down the dark hallway. There should have been a strip of light under the bathroom door, but there wasn't. Fanny wasn't on the toilet. Where was she? With a beating heart, Fips

141

walked down the stairs. He felt like a child spying on Christmas Eve. Bad boy. If Dad caught him, he would … But he heard Dad's snoring coming from the bedroom. Everything was fine.

It was too quiet downstairs. And dark. Fips heard something nonetheless. Rattling breath. Why didn't she finally die?

Fips went to the kitchen. It smelled of food. And shit. The woman hung crookedly from the chair. He turned on the light and flinched at her sight. But he had known it. In the end they had removed her cheeks, because dad loved that tender meat so much. Now you could look inside her and see her tongue twitching. Her eyes were closed.

Poor girl. Poor, poor girl. Why don't you die?

Was it the will to survive or a coincidence? Maybe everything was coincidence. The whole fucking life … After all, you couldn't choose any of it. Otherwise Fips wouldn't be here. And neither would the woman.

He approached her with his heart pounding in his mouth. She looked like a zombie, not a human being. Nevertheless, she was alive. And tomorrow was another holiday.

Fips noisily sucked in the air. It would be easy and go really fast. Nobody would know. Then they would believe she had just died. Who would blame her?

Fips raised his hand and looked down at the woman who was no longer a woman. She didn't even have breasts. Only bloody holes and raw meat. She stank miserably because shit leaked out of her all the time. Was that the process of dying?

142

Fips's hand shook, but it would serve its purpose because she had almost sighed out her soul anyway. He wouldn't need much strength. He put his hand on the woman's face, covered nose and mouth, felt warm, damp breath, took the second hand, pressed tightly, and felt nothing.

Nothing at all.

***

Fanny loved his kisses, but the thought of where his cock had been just before disgusted her! She angrily shoved her brother away. She had convinced herself that she lusted for it and that she could somehow suppress the rest, but now that the time had come, she was unable. Although Matthias had taken a shower, she could still smell pig shit on him. And the cunt of the strange woman!

"Why did you fuck her? Why does it always have to be that way?"

Matthias seemed confused. He shrugged and let go of her. "You know it. It's part of it."

"Says who?" she asked. "Dad?"

Matthias said nothing, because the answer was obvious. It was Dad. It would always be him. Because they were not his children but his goddamn slaves!

Fips was right, she thought: it had to stop!

"Do you really want to dance to his tune for the rest of your life?"

Matthias shrugged again. Could he do anything else?

"Do you really enjoy it?"

Why didn't this motherfucker answer?

"That's not normal! That ... that's all so sick!"

Matthias finally agreed with her. "Yes. It's sick." He sighed, reached out his hand, pinched her nipple. "That too! Right?"

At first Fanny didn't know what he was talking about. Or did she just not want to understand it? *What do you mean?* she wanted to ask, but the words got stuck in her throat. Because it was clear what Matthias was going for. They were brother and sister, damn it!

Matthias's hand shot forward again, grabbed her right breast, and squeezed so hard that it hurt. With the other hand, he grabbed his half-erect penis and started rubbing it as he twisted Fanny's nipple to the threshold of pain. She thought of knocking his hand away but didn't. Tears ran down her face, but the tingling was there nonetheless. In her crotch and deep inside her guts.

"It's sick!" Matthias gasped between clenched teeth. "And it's hot!"

Fanny leaned back and groaned. The pain was exquisite. Sweet and bitter. Sick and horny ...

"Do you like it, sis?"

Meanwhile, blood was flowing, and Matthias bent over to suck it away. Stars exploded behind Fanny's closed lids. Sister. Sick and horny ... Matthias grabbed her face and forced her to look at him.

"That's us, isn't it?" he moaned.

His lips touched hers, his tongue was hard and demanding. And then he bit her. Fanny reared up, tasted her own blood. Matthias paused and looked at her.

His lips were covered with blood. It looked like lipstick. Fanny sighed and cried, but she stretched her arms far over her head. She wanted him to continue and surrendered herself to him.

Sick and horny …

Matthias grabbed his sister, beat and scratched her, turned her around, took her brutally from behind.

Sick and horny … that's the way they had learned it. They wanted it that way.

***

"Fuckin' shit! What the fuck is that asshole doing?"

Fips took his blood- and snot-smeared hands from the woman's face and turned around. Matthias and Fanny stood in the doorway. Matthias and Fanny. Why the two of them? Why here and now? Where did they come from? Fanny's hair was messed up. And was that blood on her upper lip?

Fips didn't have time to think about it, because Matthias whirled toward him like a dervish, grabbed him by the shoulders, and threw him to the floor.

Fips hit his shoulder painfully. Before he could get on his feet again, his brother had already started kicking him in the ribs. Fips didn't make a sound. All he could do was bend over and moan quietly.

Fanny's voice sounded from the background. She stood next to the woman. "She's dead."

Thank you, God! Fips thought. *Thank you, thank you, thank you!* That was worth it.

"The little shit wanted to play God," Matthias yelled and kicked even harder.

Fips tried to roll up like a hedgehog. As small as possible. The pain was breathtaking and came over him in pulsating waves. It cracked again and again, clearly audibly. A rib. And two. How many ribs did one have?

"Get Dad," he heard his brother scream.

"Are you sure?" Fanny's voice sounded weak and anxious.

Where had she been? And why was Matthias with her?

"Of course." Matthias drooled. He gave neither himself nor Fips a break. His kicks came quickly and unerringly. "Come on! Do it!"

"Won't he ask why we ..." She didn't talk any further. Because she didn't know what to say or because it was obvious?

For Fips it was not obvious. Quite the opposite. Despite the pain, he still wondered where she had been. And why with Matthias? What should be obvious then? Matthias was a pig, just like Dad. But Fanny was different! Right? She had to be different, because otherwise nothing would ever make sense again!

"Fuck it," Matthias nagged breathlessly. "This isn't about us!"

Us? Why did he say that? What kind of us?

Fips tried to catch a glimpse of his sister and neglected his protection for a moment. Matthias's foot hit him directly under the chin, and this time there weren't little stars. This time all the lights went out.

When Fips came to, the lower half of his face felt like a balloon. He touched it carefully, but the pain made his skull explode, so he took his hand away.

What had happened?

He wanted to turn his head. It hurt too much. He could only lie still and stare into the darkness. With each breath he felt his cracked ribs. It was pitch dark. And damp. He lay on hard ground.

The potato cellar?

Oh no, please …!

Fips wanted to whine, scream, and somehow draw attention to himself, but the pain was as hot and billowing as he imagined the fires of hell. He couldn't make a sound.

Probably not only a few of his ribs, but also his jaw was broken. And they just left him down here? What did that mean? Would he die? For a strange woman who was already half dead? Was that the gratitude? Why did he have to be so stupid? This martyrdom brought him nothing but suffering!

Fips sat up. Dizziness struck him, and the pain was so overwhelming that he stumbled again to the brink of fainting. He leaned against the damp wall and breathed as calmly as he could. Slowly it got better.

He lay his head back and closed his eyes. Better. At least a little. Did they know how badly injured he was? Did they care? And Fanny? Fips couldn't remember what had happened after Matthias had kicked him.

The abused woman had died. He had redeemed her. He was still happy that he'd done it.

Matthias and Fanny had suddenly appeared, apparently from outside. Together. In the middle of the night. Why? What united them? Until recently, Fips had thought he was her favorite brother and that they had a special connection, but if she was hanging out with Matthias at night, he probably had to rethink that.

Matthias wasn't like him at all. He was like Dad. Maybe even worse. What did Fanny want from him? Or had he forced her? Surely Matthias was capable of doing that. In Fips's opinion, there was nothing Matthias wouldn't do.

Was Fanny having an affair with him? Her own brother? This goddamn sadist? Fips tried to imagine it. Hadn't he just recently wondered about Fanny's cravings? Did she ever have a boyfriend, or had she thought of one?

Of course, she had!

Why Matthias? Why him of all people?

She probably should have taken me!

No! They were brother and sister, and it wasn't right!

Matthias is her brother too.

Yes, he was. Good God, he was! Was there really no trace of normalcy in this damn family of psychos? Was it even possible to keep your mental health here? Fips had convinced himself that he had succeeded, but that wasn't true. He was just as crazy as the rest. This family was freakier than a nest of shithouse rats! Maybe it would be better to die down here.

Fips didn't want to know what was going on up there or why his beloved sister was hanging out with the biggest asshole ever. The fact that at least everything remained in the family was no consolation for Fips. Quite the opposite. Fanny had meant everything to him. He would have walked through fire for her. What had she done?

Fips felt tears on his cheeks. He couldn't wipe them off because touching his face hurt too much. He had Matthias to thank for that. And Fanny. Especially her, because she had pretended to be on his side while secretly fucking Matthias. Fips didn't want to imagine it, but he knew it was true.

Perhaps his sister was even in love. It didn't matter that Matthias was her brother. Nothing mattered in this family.

Fips tried to breathe the pain away somehow. He wished he could faint again. So deep and dark that he would never wake up from it. No more thinking, not feeling anything anymore, no longer being ...

What came over him was a dreamless sleep. At least ...

***

It hurt Fanny's heart when she watched Dad and Matthias dragging the unconscious Fips into the cellar. The lower half of his face was strangely contorted, and he was bleeding from his mouth. She wanted to stop them. If only she'd known how.

She loved Fips and felt terribly sorry for him. It had been stupid of him to suffocate this woman, but he must have done it with best intentions. Fips always had good intentions. That was exactly his problem.

Fanny loved not only Fips but also Matthias. The way he touched her, the taste of his kisses, the smell of his skin ... She didn't think she could live without him. It wouldn't be nice without Fips, but it would still be easier than losing Matthias. Fips wasn't strong and self-confident. Instead, he did the wrong thing again and again, helping no one. Not even this poor woman, who was half dead anyway. Surely she would have died tonight without his help. Then he wouldn't be sitting in the cellar again, seriously injured this time. Fanny had asked for permission to bring him some water, but Dad had forbidden it. He wanted to decide tomorrow what to do with Fips. That's all he said. Instead, he groped the dead woman until his trousers were about to burst.

Fanny and Matthias left the room when Dad undressed himself. Not even Matthias wanted to see that.

He accompanied Fanny to her room.

"What if he dies?" she whispered hoarsely.

"Then it's his own fault," Matthias said, shrugging. That was his favorite gesture.

"But he ..."

"Besides, you don't die that fast. You saw that slut, didn't you?"

Fanny had seen it before and most of the time had wished it would go faster. Only not now. Not with Fips.

"Do you think I'll be allowed to take care of him tomorrow?"

"I don't know," Matthias replied. "Is it so important?"

"He's our brother. You should care about him."

"He's an asshole, Fanny. He always has been. He doesn't belong here at all."

"I think he does."

Matthias laughed disparagingly. "Try your luck, sister. I won't lift a finger for that moron. He screwed up."

Fanny nodded. It was probably better if the two brothers wouldn't meet again so soon.

"It's a shame you only think of Fips after a night like this." Matthias grabbed a strand of her hair and let it slide over his fingers.

He was so close that Fanny felt his breath. She wanted to press herself against him and hug him, but that seemed too risky. Someone could come around the corner at any moment. And in the middle of the night? Everything was possible in this house.

They gazed into each other's eyes.

"You are still my girl, aren't you?" Matthias's voice was nothing more than a whisper.

Fanny nodded. Where had her breath gone? Suddenly he grabbed her already-abused breast. The pain was sweet. Fanny moaned softly. Her crotch was pounding.

"Right?" He didn't let go but squeezed and pinched.

"Yes." Fanny gasped. "Yes, I am!"

Matthias's other hand moved to her crotch. Painful. Sick. Horny. "Show me!" He pushed her through the open door into her room.

Here and now? Was he serious? He probably only dared because Dad would be busy in the kitchen for a while.

Fanny was melted wax in his hands. The more he hurt her, the more desperately she wanted him. And she got him. Again and again. Until it burned and bled. Sick and horny.

***

Mitzi, who was called *Pussy* at school, woke up on Christmas Day because her stomach hurt. Did she eat too much? She was always so careful.

Maybe she got her period. Was it time again? Mitzi hated her period. She hated having bellyaches and also hated her body!

It always hurt in the wrong places or felt good in the wrong places. Did her siblings have this problem? Fanny maybe? Mitzi would never have dared to ask. The reason why she didn't want to eat meat anymore had nothing to do with youthful obsession with slenderness. In fact, Mitzi didn't give a fuck about her looks. She knew she was ugly. She didn't need stupid classmates to write it on the blackboard or yell it in her face. After all, she looked in the mirror from time to time, even if reluctantly. Fanny had been lucky. She slightly resembled Mama but had no similarities with Dad.

Mitzi, on the other hand, was a carbon copy of her father. Rough and coarse. She hated her reflection. The misshapen face, the dumpy body with the small breasts and the hanging labia. Her limbs were short and thick and clumsy. Her hair was stringy no matter how often she washed it. Mitzi couldn't imagine that there would ever be a man who would voluntarily touch her. She had a sharp and piercing feeling of envy every time she had to watch Dad and her brothers abusing these strange women. Mitzi had no pity for the women who, despite all their suffering, were allowed to experience something that she herself would never be granted: they were desired.

Sometimes she imagined that Dad or one of her brothers—no matter which one—would sneak into her room at night. She would have to be very quiet and take off her nightgown so that he could touch her everywhere. Maybe it would hurt a little at first, but that would be okay. Mitzi would clamp her teeth together and let it happen. She would be a good girl. So well-behaved …

But all that came were those damn stomach pains! A body like hers had to hurt! How could you be so ugly and useless? If Dad had asked her to, Mitzi would have voluntarily gone to the attic to lay down in the dirty straw. They would never need a new woman again. Mitzi would have been happy to serve her family in this way, no matter how brutal the men were. That was part of it. Women were made to endure that. They could absorb the pain as well as the seeds the men shot into them.

153

Whenever Mitzi ate the flesh of a dead woman, she imagined that it was part of herself, but instead of disgust, this thought aroused her, but it was an arousal she couldn't handle. So at some point she stopped eating meat. Instead, she watched Dad and her brothers and imagined what it would be like to be fucked by them. Day and night. From the front and from behind. Then her useless body would finally be good for something.

Her door remained closed. But Mitzi sneaked out to use the toilet. The abdominal pain must have had some reason for being there. When she stepped into the hallway, screams struck her ears. Something seemed to be going on down in the kitchen. She recognized Matthias's voice. He sounded angry. Fanny seemed to be there too. She spoke very softly. Dad's vocal cords rumbled like a thunderstorm. What were they doing down there?

Mitzi hesitated. Finally she retreated to her room because she didn't want to be caught listening. She waited for almost half an hour until it was quiet again. Her stomach hurt even more. She desperately had to use the toilet. She opened the door again. This time, silence. Mitzi made her way to the bathroom, past her sister's room.

She froze. Was that a moan? Quiet screams. The wheezing of a man. Breathlessly, Mitzi pressed her ear against the wood. Fanny's mattress squeaked, and that other noise ... did it sound like that when meat slapped their meat? Mitzi barely dared to breathe.

Fanny was having sex. But with whom? Mitzi touched herself without really noticing. Was her pussy so wet because she had her period?

Actually, she didn't care who her sister was fucking. Dad, Andi, Matthias, or Fips—Mitzi would let them all have their way with her, if only they allowed it. In any case, someone wanted Fanny. Sure, she was pretty and had a great figure. Her hair was a dream.

Maybe you can also be a little sexy if you try. After all, the other women aren't as pretty as Fanny either. It's not just about the looks.

With trembling hands Mitzi pulled her nightgown over her head. She was naked underneath. Her crotch felt wet and slimy. In fact, there was some blood on her fingers. Now she knew where the abdominal pain came from. Mitzi kept touching herself. She moaned. The sex noises in her sister's room grew louder and louder.

Finally Mitzi plucked up her courage and opened the door.

***

"What the fuck?" Matthias kept thrusting into Fanny, who was crouching in front of him while he stared at his younger sister. Had she lost her mind? Mitzi was stark naked—truly not a pretty sight—and she fumbled with one hand between her legs.

"Are you crazy?" Matthias barked. Although the sight of his younger sister didn't necessarily excite him for various reasons, he was still close to his climax and

155

Mitzi rolled her eyes downward. That couldn't be true!

"Mitzi? Are you listening to me?"

She looked at him, although it didn't seem easy for her. Suddenly Matthias could smell her. A blend of blood and unwashed pussy. Usually smells didn't bother him. He'd to deal with them since childhood and wasn't too squeamish when it came to dirty female bodies. But this was his sister, damn it! His little sister!

"Do you get it?" He pressed his fingers into her cheeks until it was painful for him, but Mitzi didn't complain. Did she enjoy it? In any case, she smiled and nodded obediently.

"You can fuck me if you want. Just like her. I won't scream, I promise."

Matthias shook his head, let her go, and backed away. Suddenly he became unpleasantly aware of his nakedness. The little bitch devoured his body with her eyes.

"I mean it!" Was there a tremble in his voice? In the background, Fanny cleared her throat and rustled with the bedding. Had she heard it too?

Mitzi came closer, one hand between her plump thighs, the other kneading her left breast, which was slightly smaller than her right one and littered with big birthmarks. Matthias had never seen his sister like this before. And he would have begged God to spare him this sight if it had not already been too late.

"What's wrong with you? Don't you like me? It doesn't matter what I look like. I'll do anything you want."

"I want you to leave!" Matthias shouted. If it continued like this, Dad would become aware of this ugly little intermezzo. Matthias didn't want to think about what would happen. Of course, Dad would blame him. When the going got tough, it was always the boys' fault.

"Get out of here"

"I only want you to touch me like you touch her." She spat the last word like a lump of snot in Fanny's direction, who was no longer laughing.

Mitzi sounded desperate and close to tears, but Matthias felt disgust instead of pity. It would rather snow in hell before he touched the little slut.

Mitzi reached out to him. There was indeed blood and some slimy stuff on her fingers, and Matthias didn't even want to know what it was. "Go away, Mitzi! And if you tell anybody, I'll kill you!"

While he was still talking, Matthias realized he was really serious about it. He would wring the neck of that ugly little bitch. Sister or not. In this house, it was of minor importance.

"But I …"

"You heard your brother!" Fanny interrupted.

Finally! Where had she been? Why did it take her so long to say something?

Fanny yelled, "Get the hell out of here!"

Mitzi cringed, as if her sister's words carried more weight than her brother's. Of course, Fanny didn't have a feisty sausage hanging between her legs. Mitzi took a last look at her brother's before she turned away.

"And not a single word to anybody!" Fanny's didn't tremble. Perhaps that had something to do with her missing sausage?

Mitzi didn't answer. She gave a snide grunt.

Matthias noticed that her butt, which was also littered with birthmarks, was probably the most attractive part of her body. It was the last thing he saw of his little sister before she slammed the door behind her.

Matthias turned to Fanny. His knees were trembling. "What was *that?*"

Fanny shrugged. "Our little sister is growing up." She grinned.

Matthias didn't think it was funny.

***

The next morning Helga was in the kitchen, preparing and packaging the remaining meat. She had slept soundly that night and hadn't noticed anything out of order. She did notice that her husband had been away for a while. When he crawled back into bed, he smelled of fresh blood. But Helga didn't ask where he'd been or what he'd done. She didn't even ask herself this question.

"Fips screwed up again," he growled in the darkness.

Helga didn't have to know anything more. She didn't want to know even that much. A short time later her husband was snoring deeply. Sometimes he sounded like an animal.

Before she began her work the next morning, she opened the hatch to the cellar and looked down with a flashlight. She had to check.

Her youngest son lay rolled up on his side like a newborn. His breath was jerky, and when he raised his head with a groan, she could tell his jaw was broken. If he didn't get treatment, it would disfigure him forever and make eating a challenge.

Of course, she didn't know if Peter would let him live long enough. The way Fips had been battered, he must have done more this time than just offer the woman water or gum.

Fips whimpered miserably, like an animal in a trap. He must have been in severe pain, and he needed water.

He wouldn't get it from her.

"Lay back down!" Helga hissed. She backed away and closed the hatch.

His whimpering was so quiet you could hardly hear it.

If Fips died, she'd cut up his body just like all the others. She knew that. Still, she suddenly felt a sting in her chest. Every breath hurt. If she went back to work quickly and moved swiftly, she might be able to spend time with the pigs after dinner. This thought cheered Helga up. So she started to work and (almost) didn't think about her son in the cellar.

***

After dinner, Peter wiped his hand over his greasy mouth and burped unrestrainedly before he spoke to his family.

"You know what Fips has done. He wanted to play God. Let's see if God can still help him. Get him out of the cellar and take care of him. If he survives, it's probably how it should be."

Andi put away his napkin and rose as if on command. "I'll bring him upstairs."

Peter's gaze drilled into Matthias's face. "You don't want to help your brother?"

Rather reluctantly, Matthias stood up.

"The women will take care of the rest."

Fanny and Mitzi nodded. Peter didn't notice their tight-lipped faces and dark eyes. He had something else in mind after the meal. A girl was waiting for him in the attic.

***

Susan didn't know how long it had been since Clara and she were separated. She'd been alone again for quite a while, long enough to turn her thirst into a burning, overwhelming desire. There was hunger, somewhere deep inside, where it ate its way into her entrails like a mad rodent, but Susan could handle it. Same with the pain in her abdomen, her vagina, and her anus. It only took a little practice to push all this into the far corner of consciousness. But thirst couldn't be so easily dispelled. It was like a nasty little dog that had bitten into her throat and just wouldn't let go.

That's how her thirst felt. Like a slow, burning death, dull and senseless. If Susan had been smart, she wouldn't have left her safe place. Clara had certainly stayed there until the end. But what did that mean *until the end*? Was she really dead? Susan wished it for her, because when she'd last seen Clara, Susan realized there was no hope for her. The best thing that could happen to Clara was a quick, merciful death. But this family did not give the impression as if they would grant something like that to their victims. These people were worse than animals. Monsters.

And the most brutal of all monsters finally came back to her, because despite all her fear and despair, Susan longed for his arrival. Her throat pounded greedily as the lord of the house opened his pants and took out the short thick penis. She opened her mouth and drank. She didn't feel or taste anything. She only felt this infinite relief of not having to die of thirst and tried not to waste a drop.

The old guy helped her by shoving himself deep into her mouth and holding her head. When he came, Susan swallowed it just as greedily as she had swallowed the urine.

Satisfied, he stroked her head and said, "Good girl." Again and again.

This time he left without hitting her. Susan was relieved. A feeling of gratitude flooded her senses. She just had to be a good girl, and then everything would be all right. The main thing was that she no longer had to suffer from thirst. You could get used to the taste of urine—shocking but true. The only thing that was still bothering her was the uncertainty about the fate of her friend. She had not dared to ask her tormentor about Clara. Maybe he would have become angry and hurt her again.

Susan was happy to finally fall asleep without thirst or new pain. Only the hunger was much more noticeable than before. Maybe one of the women would come to her later and bring her something. After all, the master of the house had called her a good girl. That was supposed to mean something, right? Susan was pretty sure that everyone here danced to his tune. For better or for worse.

Clara probably wasn't alive anymore. Susan had to come to terms with that. But maybe she could manage somehow. First of all, she had to gather her strength and get out of here.

Susan had no idea how—every attempt would fail because of the chains—but she didn't want to give up yet. She only wanted to pretend, so that the bad man thought she was a good girl. She would do anything, no matter how humiliating or disgusting it was. As long as she didn't end up as a piece of meat in that terrible kitchen. Like Clara at the worst Christmas dinner ever.

Susan couldn't understand how this cannibal family had been able to live undiscovered so far. They'd probably been torturing and murdering women long before Clara's and her kidnapping. The house may have been remote; there were certainly no close neighbors and no one who happened to get lost here, but how had they been able to keep it up? Didn't the children go to school? Didn't they have jobs? Was such a thing possible in a well-developed and densely populated country like Germany?

Susan might have imagined such atrocities in a remote corner of America, where you'd drive for hours along a prairie without meeting a soul. Even there it would be difficult in the long run to keep such monstrosities secret, but here in Germany? Susan just couldn't get it into her head. After all, there had to be a reason why all the slasher movies like *The Chainsaw Massacre* or *Charlie's Farm* were set in vast Texas or in the Australian outback. Only Clara and Susan had managed to come to Europe and meet the really dangerous hillbillies. And on the cursed Oktoberfest, where there was a huge mass of people. How much bad luck could you have?

Surely their families had never expected such a nightmare to happen to them in a manageable country like Germany.

However, Susan didn't want to think about her family. That just hurt too much. If she ever got out of here alive, sooner or later she would have to face Clara's parents and tell them the terrible truth. Even the thought of it made her brain soft and her limbs weak. She almost wished for a quick, painless death, followed by final redemption. *Just don't think anymore, don't torture your head anymore, don't have any worries or feelings anymore.* Trying to understand the whole thing hurt too much.

How could a pretty girl like Fanny be so heartless? How could a mother allow her children to turn into such monsters? How could a man who was a father himself do such things to the children of others?

Susan didn't understand it, and thinking about it drove her crazy. It was much easier to turn off all thoughts and just let it happen. Just be a good girl.

So on this second Christmas day she lay down in the straw. She closed her eyes and tried to sleep.

The Good Girl

It was already mid-January before Fips was finally able to experience a morning where he didn't want to scream out in pain. Two more weeks passed before he was again able to eat a bit of oatmeal with a spoon instead of liquid food through a straw. Speaking was still difficult.

Since this would be a problem with school, Dad had deregistered him. He was allegedly going to visit another school. Would anyone check it out? Fips wasn't sure. He wasn't a child anymore. At seventeen, there was no compulsory schooling. Of course, one would wonder, but he doubted whether that would be enough to take any further steps.

So he stayed home for a while. Maybe he just wasn't up for it any more, like many young people his age. Maybe his family would claim that he had run away and put him back in the potato cellar if someone actually came to check. The fact was, he had almost died and would never be able to let himself be seen anywhere again. His ribs would heal, but his jaw would grow together completely crooked and would probably have to be broken and straightened again if he wanted to look like halfway normal again. Nobody here would do that for him. Fips was supposed to be grateful that he was still alive, even though he would likely never speak properly again, let alone eat.

Was he grateful?

He was glad the pain had subsided. For weeks he had swallowed ibuprofen like candy without any noticeable improvement. He could finally sleep properly again and concentrate on a book or a TV show without being distracted by the constant throbbing in his lower jaw.

Fips wouldn't get used to the sight of it so soon, though. If at all. His average teenage face had turned into a monster face. At least he saw in the mirror what he had felt inside him for so long.

The monster had finally gained the upper hand.

The only advantage of all this was the privilege of being allowed to stay alone. Dad had never asked him to eat in the kitchen or even sent him to the attic to do what monsters did. Was the second woman still alive? Fips didn't really know what he should wish for her. He didn't even know what he wanted for himself.

That evening he talked about it with Mitzi, who brought him some semolina.

"Is the woman in the attic still alive?"

Mitzi's acne was just as burning red as his own. Today, however, Fips had other problems.

Mitzi nodded. She didn't feel like talking. Lately she had become even more withdrawn than before. Fips sometimes wondered if she might have a secret. Dirty and gloomy, like all the secrets in this house. At school they had certainly asked about him. What had she told them? After all, the fate of her entire family could depend on these answers. Was she aware of that? Was that why she seemed so depressed, or did Fips take himself too seriously? It probably had nothing to do with him.

"Why do you want to know?" Mitzi asked without much interest. "You wanna see her?"

"What? No! What makes you think that?"

Mitzi shrugged, still seeming completely unimpressed, yet she suddenly had a sparkle in her eye that Fips didn't like very much. "After all, it's not like you'll be able to get another one."

What? What had she said? It felt like she hit him in the head with a hammer. It also hit Fips in another spot: right in his heart. Why was she so mean? After all, she was his sister, and she wasn't exactly the epitome of beauty either! Fips stared at his porridge. There was a second bowl with some fresh compote next to it, but he no longer had any appetite.

"Why do you say that?" He felt his hot tears.

"Because it's true," Mitzi replied without any emotion. "In any case, the woman is still alive."

"It's not my fault that I look like this," Fips whined, although he didn't really want to complain. Especially not here and in front of this heartless cow.

Mitzi gave him a look that almost seemed compassionate. Or was it superiority? "You're a bit hard to understand," Mitzi said.

Really? As if he hadn't known that! "I can't help it," Fips cried, although he knew he would hardly be understood.

Mitzi shrugged. With the expression of complete indifference on her face, she said something that made the blood in Fips's veins freeze, and his heart slid out of his chest.

"I would take you anyway. Your face is ugly, but it's more about the body, right?"

Fips stared at her. He had known for a long time that his family was completely crazy and fucked up, but this offer from his own sister left him speechless. That was just too much.

"You probably can't do much with your mouth anymore. The rest should still work," Mitzi continued, doing the unbelievable: she pulled down the waistband of her pants so far that Fips could see the base of her pubic hair. "If you'd like a taste …"

The shock was so great that Fips's tears dried up.

"There's nothing to it," Mitzi said while she made a hand disappear in her pants. She pulled it out again and held her fingers under his nose. They smelled slightly sour, but not unpleasant.

Nevertheless, Fips turned away. "What is this all about, Mitzi? Are you crazy?"

"Do I smell so bad?"

"That's not what it's about!"

"What else?"

"You're my sister!"

Mitzi wrinkled her nose. "Fanny is Matthias's sister, right?"

And there it was. The one bad truth that Fips had suppressed all the time. Although on some level he'd known. Of course.

"And they do everything that man and woman can do. Well, if you feel like it …" Her fingers were in

Fips's face again. She stroked his lips and left a taste that made Fips shiver.

He forced himself to leave his tongue in his mouth and wipe it off with his hand instead. "Stop it," he said.

"Think about it, Fips. You won't get any other offers. And at least I'm a woman."

At least a woman …

Fips had to think of Fanny, who'd hardly been around since they'd brought him up from the cellar. She fucked that damn sadist Matthias! Fips had never been anything special to her. He'd only imagined it. Now that he was in such bad condition, she hadn't visited even once to comfort him. But it was her lover who had done this to him. Fips hated them both! He hated them with all his heart and all his remaining strength.

He held back Mitzi, who was about to turn away, shoved his hand into her pants, and put his lips close to her ear. Fips held his little sister tight because she was the only support he still had.

***

"Mitzi?"

She looked up from the magazine she'd flipped through, lying on her belly on the bed. Actually, she should have done something for school, but who cared? Just like Fips, she wouldn't be going there much longer. Her soul felt no less disfigured than her brother's face. There was no real future for members

170

of the Koller family. At least no future that dealt with anything normal.

Fanny stood in the door, looking as pretty as always. Mitzi hated her for it. If she looked like Fanny, she would never have needed to kiss her disfigured brother's ass.

Fips intended to turn against the family, while all she wanted was a little appreciation. Now she had him in the palm of her hand because she knew his secret. But Fips wasn't allowed to know that. He thought she was on his side because she wanted to fuck him, but sex and loyalty were two different things.

For a bit of fun, she pretended to be willing to help him. He planned to free the woman in the attic and escape with her. But in reality, Mitzi would never stab her family in the back. Despite all envy, she even kept the hanky-panky between Fanny and Matthias to herself. Fips knew about it, but Fips wasn't the problem because his own secrets were a lot weightier. He had no interest in exposing Fanny and Matthias, because if his plans could be realized, everything that this family had ever represented would break anyway.

It wouldn't come to that, of course. Not if Mitzi could prevent it. But a bit of fun was okay. She felt ready. Fips knew exactly how to touch a woman, she had to admit. They hadn't gone to extremes yet, but the little taste definitely made her want more.

In her wildest dreams, Mitzi could not have imagined how horny the hand of a man in her panties could make her feel. She had given Fips a taste of herself, and she knew he'd enjoyed it. He still showed some resistance, but that would end. Mitzi was sure of that.

Life was simply too short to go without such moments, and if she did it right, Fips might even belong to her someday. What else did he have to look forward to, with that face?

But of course she would first have to make him get rid of his silly ideas. If he refused to satisfy her, she would blackmail him by threatening to tell Dad. He still thought he could get her on his side with a few favors—not that he wouldn't like it himself—but Mitzi would soon turn the tables on him and teach him better. At the latest, after they slept together for the first time. That would give her another advantage.

The question was: What did Fanny want from Mitzi? She never came to her room.

"We have to talk to you."

Mitzi raised her eyebrows. "Oh yeah?"

"Yes. Matthias is already in the hut. We're undisturbed there."

The hut? That was more than weird. Why did they want to meet her in the hut? Mitzi hadn't been there for years. As a little girl she'd found it exciting to play out there. She even been there with Fips, but never with Fanny or Matthias. Nowadays the little cabin was only used as a storage space. Mitzi didn't know if anyone went there at all. Surely it was rotten and in ruins by now. She'd never seen anyone going to the hut except to repair it.

Maybe Fanny and Matthias were out there more often. But Mitzi couldn't imagine that it was too comfortable there at the moment. First you had to stomp through the knee-high snow for a quarter of an hour, and then you froze your ass off in the ramshackle shed. Who wanted to do something like that?

"Why the hut?" she asked her sister.

"Because you can't talk in private in this house," Fanny replied impatiently.

Only now Mitzi noticed how rushed she looked. With sweaty strands of hair and hectic red spots on her cheeks. She was already wearing a winter jacket and cap.

"Come on! It's important!"

Could be a trap, Mitzi thought, but that was nonsense. What kind of trap? There was no reason for that. *Maybe they're still afraid that I might tell on them.*

Was that possible? Wouldn't she have done that by now? Perhaps it would really make sense to talk about the subject again. Mitzi could calm them down. She had completely different thoughts in her head than to betray her siblings to Dad. Her head was full of Fips and everything she wanted to do with him, whether he liked it or not. It could never hurt to have an ace or two up your sleeve.

She put the magazine aside—the latest issue of *Bravo*, because she was a teenager, after all—and got up.

"Put on something warm. It's freezing outside."

Mitzi wondered whether she should ask again why they had chosen the hut as their meeting place.

Because nobody can hear me screaming there.

Bullshit! Besides, she went along to sort it out. It was okay for Fanny and Matthias to know that her interest had switched to Fips. She was no longer offended by Matthias's rejection. She was probably just too young for him. One couldn't blame him for this attitude. Maybe sex with the older sister somehow felt morally acceptable to him. If necessary, he could blame Fanny, who was older. With Mitzi it was different. After all, a big brother could not escape his responsibility so easily.

So Mitzi and her sister would stomp to that damn hut and settle this once and for all. Basically, she was happy. It shouldn't be between them any longer.

She grabbed a thick jacket and her favorite scarf and followed her sister downstairs. They didn't meet anyone on the way to the front door, but they heard Mama with the clattering dishes in the kitchen. Fips was in his room, which he had rarely left since his beating. Dad was up in the attic again, and Andi wouldn't be back from work for a few hours. Nobody saw the two sisters leave the house. Only their footsteps revealed where they were going, but these would soon disappear in the increasing snowstorm.

***

The hut was snowed in and almost as dilapidated as Mitzi had imagined it. The mattress with the rumpled blankets lying in a corner also matched her imagination. Fanny and Matthias actually came here to have sex. Only in winter, they had to find another place. It

174

was so cold that even Mitzi couldn't imagine feeling lusty here. She noticed an almost empty box of beer and several burned candles before she realized Matthias wasn't here.

"Where …" Mitzi had just turned halfway to Fanny behind her when she was suddenly hit on the head.

She briefly saw Matthias, who had probably just come in through the door, holding a hammer or an axe in his hand. The next moment a red veil fell over Mitzi's eyes. She staggered backward.

Fanny was suddenly no longer to be seen. Matthias quickly approached her and hit her again.

Mitzi raised her hands to protect her face, but Matthias aimed for her head. With the next hit, something red poured into Mitzi's eyes, and her knees buckled. She tried to look at her brother and say something as long as she still could. The only thing that came out was a lot of garbled sounds. She could no longer plead or explain anything because she'd soon die in this cold old hut.

Matthias unerringly bashed her skull. Why had she not put on a cap? Maybe the thick fabric would have protected her a little.

But nothing protected Mitzi and her head. She had been far too stupid and naive. Couldn't she have foreseen it? Now it was too late. Too late for clarifying conversations or pleading words. She lay bent on the ground and only saw red, while the hammer crashed down on her skull again and again.

Matthias wouldn't stop until she was dead. She knew that. She would have liked to see Fanny one last time. Was there pity in her eyes? Did she look horrified or sad? Mitzi would never know. Just before her skull broke with an ugly crack, she fainted and never woke up again.

***

Blood and brain matter stained Matthias's work boots when he finally stopped. Fanny pressed both hands to her mouth. She hadn't imagined it to be this bad. Maybe she would have to vomit.

Matthias threw the hammer next to his sister's dead body. He breathed heavily and looked exhausted. The little puffs of white clouds that came out of his mouth looked almost surreal to Fanny. She wanted to ask if Mitzi was dead, but that question was unnecessary. The girl's skull was exposed, and her brain was spilling out. One of her eyes was bulging unnaturally far from the socket. She reminded Fanny of the dolls she had broken when she was a child.

"We shouldn't have done that," she whispered, wondering about her own clouds of breath. The air didn't feel that cold. Or was she just sweating because she was about to lose her mind? "I don't think she would have told anyone about us."

"And how many times has she been with Fips lately?" Matthias snarled at her. "You said yourself that they were up to something! And if Dad finds out that ... If he finds out, we can still be happy if he just beats us to cripples or smashes our faces like he did with Fips."

"You have done that to Fips!" Fanny yelled.

"Yeah, and why?" Matthias roared.

Fanny was suddenly glad he was no longer holding the hammer. They had discussed everything in advance, and it had somehow made sense, but now Mitzi lay there with her skull bashed open, and she seemed to mock them with her blood-drenched face.

The plan had been to kill her here and then bury her body and the murder weapon under the hut. Matthias had worn gloves, so there would be no trace of evidence of a crime, no clues except for any they left on the way.

But it was snowing and would soon be dark. They had kept a close eye on today's weather forecast and the time. Mama and Dad would assume Mitzi had run away. That would scare them for now. They would deregister her from school and not let anyone search for her, always hoping she wouldn't give away their secrets.

The only real danger was that someone from the school would wonder: first Fips, and now Mitzi? What was wrong with the Koller offspring? Would anyone check whether the two were registered at a new school? Would somebody ever come up with the stupid idea of sending someone from the youth welfare office?

What if? Dad could always claim they'd run away. Teenagers did that. Of course, nobody was allowed to see Fips. It would have been better if they'd buried him under the hut as well. Dad would think of something. He had always thought of something.

Otherwise he couldn't afford to keep women trapped in the attic for decades. If necessary, they would just kill the woman and Fips and feed them to the pigs before anyone became suspicious. Fanny was pretty sure Dad would do that. He had already left it to fate whether his youngest son lived or died. After all, he knew Fips would never really be part of it all. And Mitzi? Fanny didn't think he would miss her.

Maybe Mama would, but nobody cared what she thought anyway. Fanny suspected that her mother wasn't even interested in it anymore. She had learned to be small and unimportant and not to have any feelings or opinions of her own. You could learn *everything*. Dad always said that. Maybe you could even learn to be evil. Fanny believed that by now. She had just helped kill her own sister. If that wasn't evil …

"We should get to work," Matthias said.

Of course he was right. Mitzi's body had to vanish. They also had to make sure they got back to the house as soon as possible. Dad's questions about where they had been were unlikely to be asked today. The only hope was that he was sufficiently busy in the attic. He seemed to have taken a particular liking to this girl. He spent more time with her than with most others. He wouldn't like the fact that Mitzi's supposed escape put all this in danger. And if they were unlucky, they would feel his rage with full force. They had talked about it in advance, but it had sounded more harmless before they smashed Mitzi's skull.

"I have a feeling that was a mistake. It will break our necks," Fanny whispered. Why hadn't she thought of this far before? It seemed as if it had only taken the sight of her dead sister to bring her to her reason.

Matthias went to her and grabbed her by the shoulders. These were the hands that had killed Mitzi. Fanny suddenly knew she didn't want to be touched by him anymore. Not voluntary.

"You mustn't go crazy! Pull yourself together, Fanny!"

"Let me go!" she screamed, and to her surprise, he obeyed.

"Will you help me, or do I have to do it alone?" Matthias sounded like an offended toddler.

Fanny nodded. What else was she supposed to do? They were sitting in the same boat, and if they sank, they would sink together—like everything else.

***

Late that evening, Fips heard his father rumble in the kitchen. What had happened? There were other voices, and everyone screamed. Fips sneaked out of his room and hid on the dark landing. Now he could filter words from the screaming. It was about Mitzi.

"What shall I do? I can't even report this because we're gonna have the cops on our backs!" Dad sounded like the devil himself.

Fips imagined him having red skin and a neck about to burst, with throbbing veins like cables.

"You don't have to report this!" Matthias had rarely sounded so sheepish. "Just tell the school that she's not coming anymore. Like Fips."

"Exactly!" Fanny agreed. "Nobody cares anyway! They didn't ask about Fips, did they? And Mitzi is of age, after all."

"They *will* ask questions if Maria won't return to school either!" Dad roared.

Fips couldn't remember the last time he'd heard his sister's real name.

"And if I say she's run away, everyone will wonder why I didn't report it right away! Normal parents want to find their children again!"

Normal parents ...

Why did she run away in the first place? Fips hadn't seen any evidence of it. On the contrary ...

"Then you have to report it," Fanny suggested. She sounded anxious and desperate.

"And what if the cops show up here?"

Nobody answered. Everyone knew what would happen. It would mean the end of an era. Of their family.

This was fine with Fips. He was sure Dad wouldn't give up so easily. And if he had to leave, he would take them all with him.

"We kill the woman and wipe out all traces, then nothing can happen," Matthias said. It was typical that these words came from him.

"And what about Fips? If they see his gob, we're fucked." That was Dad. And he was absolutely right.

Looks like I'm the problem, Fips thought gloomily. Why had Mitzi run away? Especially now, when she had shown such excessive interest in Fips. When he had fingered her, she'd been blissful. As if she'd been craving it for an eternity.

"We'll hide him and say he ran away too." Fanny. Dear, sweet Fanny. Maybe she loved him after all. At least a little.

"I have a better idea." Matthias. How much Fips hated him! Fips knew exactly what was coming. Matthias would suggest his death. And Dad? He would agree out of sheer panic. What else could he do? Mitzi would probably tell what was going on here. Only by destroying all traces could they protect themselves against these accusations. And one of these traces was Fips.

"Hey, Fips! Shh!"

That came from behind him. Somewhere in the darkness of the stairwell. Fips twitched and jerked around.

Andi squatted there like a frog and had put his finger on his lips. "Shh! Come with me. You've heard enough."

What was that all about? Which side was Andi on? Why had he sneaked up on him from behind and acted like a little boy playing hide and seek? Did the others know about that? Should Andi set a trap for him?

Fips was paralyzed. What should he do? He couldn't escape Andi without running straight into the arms of the rest of his family. He had no choice but to trust his eldest brother, even though he had hardly done so before. To be honest, he hadn't thought about it at all. Andi's motives had mostly been obscure to him, and he had assumed that he was on Dad's side. After all, he was the oldest and had always done first what everyone else started later. Why exactly would the oldest and best student turn against his teacher?

Andi pulled his arm. In his excitement he looked much younger. "I want to help you, Fips! Come on!"

Fips shook his head. His confusion was just too big. Still, he let Andi pull him backward. Further into the darkness and across the hallway to Andi's room, where he hadn't been for years.

"Hide in here! And don't come out until I come back. Understand?"

"But ..."

Andi grabbed him so firmly that it hurt. "We don't have time," he hissed. "They want to kill you! You have no choice but to trust me."

Fips nodded. Andi was right. He had no choice.

"They won't expect you to be in my room. Hide in the closet."

Their eyes met, and all of a sudden Fips understood. Andi had always been on his side, but he had practiced patience and silence not to arouse suspicion. In contrast to Fips with his ill-considered actions of help, he had been smart and prudent and had waited for the right moment. Not that it had come. It was just too late for everything else.

"Okay?" Andi wanted to know.

Fips wanted to hug him. The feelings that flowed through him were so new and full of warmth that he would have loved to shout them out loud. So here he was, the ally he had always been looking for. All this time it hadn't been Fanny, but Andi.

"Thank you," he whispered in a voice suffocated with tears. Maybe because of his jaw Andi couldn't understand him, so Fips said it again: "Thanks, man."

Andi briefly pressed his shoulder and nodded. "Now get inside the closet. We'll talk later."

***

Fips didn't remember how long he'd been sitting in Andi's closet. Time turned into a snippy little dervish, and running after it made him far too tired.

First, he still heard them, and his heart almost stopped. There they were! Loud footsteps on the stairs. Buzzing voices. His family, excited and full of lust for murder. Only Mama would not be there. Mama didn't care. Nothing had ever played any role for her. Neither her husband nor her own children. She only loved her pigs, those damn filthy creatures!

It was so loud at first that Fips saw them in front of him already. How they opened the closet door and stared at him. They would drag him out and hit him. Not a family, only animals. Monsters. Fips had been one of them for a while, but that was finally over. It would also have been over if they hadn't wanted to kill him. How would they do it? With their bare hands or with a weapon? Would Mama then process him into small handy portions of meat and feed the rest to the pigs? No, this time the beasts would probably get everything. Nothing would be allowed to remain. No trace. No evidence. No more Fips. They would crush his flesh, cut up his intestines, and grind up his bones until nothing was left. Fips knew that was possible. He'd watched Mama do it often enough. As soon as a person was dead, it consisted only of meat and bones, a lot of blood, and a lot of noise about nothing. It was easy to disappear. Much easier than staying there. And they wouldn't even be sorry. Or perhaps Fanny? A bit? No, because Fanny loved Matthias. She didn't need Fips; she had never needed him. It had only been an illusion he'd created to make this terrible life a little more bearable. If he'd only known back then that Andi …

Andi! Where was he? Of course, he had to play along and couldn't risk removing his mask. He would support them in their search for Fips and hopefully lead them on the wrong track. Probably they should believe Fips had run away. Just like Mitzi. Maybe even with her. Andi would do anything to make them believe that and not look any further. What then? Fips couldn't sit in that closet forever! How could he get out of the house without being seen? And what would happen next?

Fips got a headache when he thought about it. A part of him still felt like a little boy playing hide-and-seek. Here in the closet it was dark and smelled musty, but it was comfortably warm. You could close your eyes and just let yourself drift into a world that was better and more beautiful. Fips did not know whether he would ever see such a world. He probably wouldn't have that much luck, but for the moment it was okay to dream of it.

He saw Fanny as a normal young woman with a nice husband and two cute kids. She lived in a neat row house with a well-kept garden, and her smile was finally real.

He saw Dad and Matthias in prison, where they belonged. They wore striped convicts' suits and chains on their wrists and ankles. The media would jump at the story until it got boring. Dad and Matthias would suffer and die in prison. Just as they deserved.

He saw Mama living in a pretty apartment with the lively, stylishly dressed Mitzi and who only had to look after the flowers on her little balcony instead of the stinking pigs. She'd finally started smiling and touching her daughter. When the other children came to visit, they sat in the living room drinking coffee and chattering like blabbermouths. Because Mama had not only found her smile again but her voice. And she had finally learned to love …

He saw Andi, who had also raised a family. His wife was small and dainty so that he could protect her well. His children were intelligent and popular. They could be sure of the unconditional love of their parents. Good children, they were.

He imagined the woman from the attic lying in the arms of her sobbing family. At last. She wore a colorful summer dress and had no visible scars. Together they boarded a plane that would take them wherever the sun was shining.

Fips saw himself. After a few surgeries, his face was almost like new. He was newly in love. The feeling of waking up next to her in the morning was indescribable. Sometimes they showered together and made love on the spot. Yes, the word was correct here. They loved each other and Fips knew that nothing and nobody would ever separate them. This was his fucking happy ending. And he deserved it!

But what he really saw was a dim, narrow strip of light that almost got lost in the darkness. Too little light for a happy ending. He still didn't want to give up hope. Not yet. Andi would come back and do anything to save him. He strongly believed that. His big brother would do his best, and you couldn't expect more. Whether they could still help the woman was written in the stars. Perhaps they would at least save themselves. Fips would have given everything for a good ending, but sometimes it was just too late. This family was so terribly messed up that they couldn't even have been helped in a perfect world of fairy tales.

Deep inside, Fips knew that neither he nor anyone else in his family would ever live in a pretty apartment and experience real love.

There were no happy endings for monsters.

***

Andi Koller's heart was heavy as he stomped through the snow behind his father and brother. The old man had insisted on checking out the hut after they had looked in vain for Fips in the house. Matthias didn't think this was a good idea, but the old man had discovered a few traces in the snow and couldn't be stopped. The women stayed in the house, while the men, armed with flashlights and Dad's rifle, made their way to the hut that Andi had avoided since hiding Steffi there.

Now the memories were fresh again, and he remembered her lovely round face, which in the end had turned into a terrible grimace of pain and despair. Life had not been the same ever since and never would be again.

Steffi had been his girlfriend, the only one he'd ever had, but Dad didn't care. The old man had never been interested in anything that had nothing to do with the fulfillment of his own desires.

Now he was in some real shit, though. How was he going to explain Mitzi's disappearance to the authorities? Andi was sure strangers would soon come here to take a closer look at the Koller family. Dad would have to be faster than an express train to make the woman and Fips disappear in time. And then the real fun would start. It wouldn't be easy to answer their questions and hide the truth.

This would be the perfect opportunity for Andi to finally free himself from the tyrant's grip. While Dad was still pondering how to get his head out of the noose, Andi would grab the kid and leave with him. They would go straight to the police and tell them everything. Of course, Fips's face spoke volumes.

Maybe it wasn't too late to save the woman in the attic, but Andi doubted it. He couldn't take her with him, and the old man would still have enough time to blow her lights out, even if it wasn't enough to dismember her. At least her relatives would know what had happened to her. Andi would have liked to have done more for her, but the challenge to get Fips out of here unseen was already big enough. As weak as she was, the woman would only hinder them, and in the end, nobody would benefit if all three of them were caught. That would only cause more work for the rest of the family, because there would be a third body that had to disappear.

While he trudged through the snow, Andi wondered which devil had told Mitzi to run away now, of all times. He'd never had the impression that she felt uncomfortable in the family. On the contrary. Most of the time she seemed to be bending over backwards to belong and to please Dad—or Matthias. That was strange. The others assumed the two might have made plans together, but Andi knew this wasn't true. Although he hadn't been able to ask him yet, he was pretty sure Fips had no idea where Mitzi was. It didn't make sense.

Unless … The thought was, of course, completely crazy.

Unless what? The voice in Andi's head dug deeper. That was absurd, but …

Unless she's dead, the voice said.

But why? Why would Mitzi be dead?

Maybe she was in their way, just like Fips …

The old man, however, didn't give the impression that he knew where his daughter was. Was Andi the only one who was fooling him on this beautiful winter day?

They had arrived at the hut, which looked as always. Except for the snow-covered footprints that were visible in the flashlight beam. Someone must have been here, and it didn't look like just one person.

"Perhaps he's hiding here," the old man whispered.

If he found his son, he would blow his skull off without hesitation. Andi would have bet on that.

"I'll take a look," Matthias offered, but the old man rudely held him back. "I'll do it myself!"

He entered the hut with his gun raised, only to come out a short time later with a shrug. "Someone was here, but now there's nobody around."

Andi felt relief, although he had actually known that. He would have been surprised if Mitzi had been crouched in there in this cold.

Still, there was the question of who else had been here. In any case, it hadn't been Fips. To his astonishment, Andi thought he saw a sign of relief in Matthias's face. He could hardly ask him. Matthias was a particularly cunning asshole. Andi would never be able to speak openly with him.

"What shall we do now?" Matthias wanted to know.

"We have to find him!" the old man shouted. His spittle splashed.

Andi had never seen his father so upset.

"We're going back to the house to take the car. Matthias stays there to kill the bitch. Mama and Fanny are supposed to start cutting her into pieces right away, while Matthias takes care of the attic! There must not be any trace left! No fucking DNA! Nothing at all!" The spittle splashed again.

Andi tried his luck. "Shouldn't I do that?"

"No! You stay with me!"

Andi swallowed hard. This wasn't good. Not good at all. "But ..."

"Enough! We don't have time for this shit. Matthias finishes the bitch! He's the better killer!"

How true! Andi couldn't do any more without being exposed. He had to give in and could only hope that Fips would not leave his hiding place.

Matthias grinned. The lust for murder sparkled in his eyes. "All right, Dad. So let's go!"

The old man turned to Andi. "If we don't find him, I'll probably have to answer for maltreatment. His ugly face can't be overlooked, but they have to prove we're to blame, right? If we stick together, nothing can happen."

"And what about Mitzi?"

"I don't believe she'll give us away. She must have left for other reasons."

For once they shared the same opinion.

***

Fips waited half an eternity for his brother's return. It took too long, just way too long. Had Andi's cover been blown? Had they done something to him out there in the woods? To their son and brother, to their own flesh and blood? Fips knew that neither Dad nor Matthias would shy away from such a thing. After all, they had the same plans for him.

And what about Fanny? Well, as far as Fanny was concerned, he wasn't sure, but she could probably do it. By now he thought she could do anything.

It was quiet in the house.

How long was he supposed to stay in that damn closet? Of course, he'd promised Andi he'd wait, but Andi had also promised to come back as soon as possible—and where was he now?

He could leave a message for his brother. After all, he should seize the opportunity as long as nobody was in the house, right? Maybe he could even free the woman! How about that for a happy ending?

That won't work! Never! You don't even know if you're really alone in the house!

No, but he was sure that at least the men were away. Mama had stayed in the house for sure, but she wasn't any danger. Fips didn't believe she would stand in his way if the going got tough. After all, she had never touched her children, for better or for worse. And Fanny? He could handle her!

His heart pounded so loudly in Fips's ears that he couldn't hear anything else as he slowly left the closet. It was dark outside, and the furniture was only dimly visible. With a trembling hand, Fips switched on the desk lamp. In a drawer he found notes and a few ballpoint pens. Andi liked everything to be in its place, and some would probably have called him compulsively neat.

Fips scribbled on a piece of paper: *Andi! I'm trying to help the woman. Sorry that I didn't stay! I just couldn't! Thanks for everything. Fips.*

Thanks for everything. Yes, that's how you could sum it up. Andi had already done more for Fips than any other person. He was sorry he hadn't known earlier what was really going on with his eldest brother. Then perhaps everything would have been different. Fips had always assumed Andi was on Dad's side. He had never questioned that and barely paid attention to his brother, who had carried this burden all those years alone and had suffered silently. They could have been friends. It was probably too late for that, but maybe it wasn't too late for a good deed. In Fips's case, they had all gone down the drain so far, but at least he wouldn't end up in the potato cellar anymore. This time his punishment would be final.

He put the ballpoint pen back in the drawer and put the note in the closet, where it would wait for Andi's return more patiently than Fips himself. Then he switched off the lamp and sneaked to the door.

***

Susan woke up from a restless sleep when the dusty lightbulb on the ceiling above her lit up. It was the boy who reminded her of her cousin. He hadn't been here for a long time, and he had changed. Something had happened to his face. His lower jaw seemed to have shifted, giving his features an unpleasant hardness. Was he still able to eat properly?

That's not your problem!

However, her problem was what he intended to do with her, because the pliers in his right hand were huge.

Susan sat up and pulled the blanket even tighter around her. She moaned in fear. "*Please, don't! Don't hurt me!*"

He shook his head as he kneeled in front of her.

Susan whimpered and couldn't take her eyes off the pliers. *"Please, don't! Don't do it!"*

"I don't," he said. His voice sounded warm and gentle.

Susan understood him despite the spongy pronunciation and the wrong grammar. He wouldn't hurt her. Instead, he carefully reached for the chains on her ankles.

Susan finally understood what he was going to do with the pliers! She trembled in excitement as she watched him cut the chains. He used to be one of her tormentors, but now he was her savior. The angel with the crooked face! It was too good to be true—but he really was freeing her! In a moment she would be free!

Susan was overwhelmed by her emotions. She sobbed unrestrainedly. After he removed the chains, he helped her to her feet. Susan had soft knees and could hardly stand straight, but he held her tight, which felt pleasant. Those were the first well-intentioned touches in a long time.

Suddenly she dared again to think of her family and home. Maybe it wasn't too late to return home after all. After all the horror, she would eventually rise from the ashes like a phoenix because the angel with the crooked face had come to save her. Life could be so beautiful!

Susan wrapped the blanket around her body so she wouldn't lose it. She was barefoot and would certainly freeze bitterly as soon as they were outside, but she would gladly accept that if she could only finally leave this terrible place. Hopefully he'd made sure nobody got in their way.

"You come. Shh." He put a finger to his crooked lips.

Come along and be quiet, of course. Susan understood that. She would be as quiet as a mouse. If only she would finally get away from here!

She nodded and imitated his gesture to show that she had understood. And if these were the last steps of her life, as long as they took her far enough away from here, everything would be fine.

As she let the boy lead her to the stairs—his hand felt warm and wet—she imagined her parents' faces in front of her for the first time in ages.

Mom and Dad! I'll be home soon! I'm coming home! I'm really coming home!

Suddenly the pain in her maltreated body no longer mattered. It was as if a lightning had struck her, healing and revitalizing her at the same time. Susan's head was filled with the most colorful images. Her hopelessly dried-out and foul-tasting mouth was flooded with sweet adrenaline. She held the boy's hand as if he were not one of her kidnappers but her lover. In a certain, very peculiar way, he was.

Susan was surprised her feet didn't hurt. Instead, it felt like she wasn't walking over rough wooden planks but over a sea of fluffy clouds. And her mouth tasted like cotton candy.

So that's how it felt when everything went well in the end. That was how it felt to be rescued.

***

When Fips saw his brother at the bottom of the stairs, his heart dropped into his guts. He froze, and his fingers clenched the woman's little hand, which could have belonged to a child.

She audibly sucked in breath and pressed herself against him. But how was Fips supposed to protect her? He was unarmed and hadn't even taken the damn pliers with him!

He turned to her in panic. "*Schnell! Lauf weg!*" Due to the shock, he had forgotten that she didn't understand German.

Matthias was already running up the stairs. He carried a long knife.

Although she'd probably not understood him, the woman retreated into the darkness of the corridor. She was now on her own. Just like Fips, who realized that running away made no sense. Instead, he grabbed the ancient spinning wheel that had been gathering dust by the stairs ever since he could remember. Mama's idea of decorating.

Matthias saw too late what was coming at him. He stumbled and, cursing, smashed into the spinning

195

wheel. It was foolish, but at that moment Fips thought of Sleeping Beauty, who had a fateful encounter with such a thing. However, he could imagine worse than a hundred years of sleep.

Instead of running away—as he had done for far too long—he ran toward his brother. He noticed Matthias's baffled expression and a short stabbing pain in his side, before they fell down the stairs together.

***

At the bottom of the stairs they had wedged into each other and were fighting like boys in a schoolyard. Only schoolboys rarely held knives. Again and again Fips felt the stabbing pain that would kill him sooner or later. Matthias stabbed him repeatedly in his thighs, stomach, and chest.

Fips defended himself with his hands and feet. He landed a few punches on Matthias's face and belly and tried to get a grip on him so he could push him away. Unfortunately, his hands were so damp that he slipped again and again. There was a burning pain all over his body every time Matthias scored a hit.

Fips gradually lost his strength. Matthias was above him, with a nasty grin and bloody splotches on his face.

Fips could no longer defend himself as Matthias rammed the knife up to the shaft into his abdomen. Fips stared into his brother's triumphant face and tasted blood. His hands clutched the knife handle, but he didn't have enough strength to pull it out. He would die anyway.

"There you have it," Matthias growled.

Mama suddenly showed up in Fips's blurred and colorless vision. Or had she been there all the time? He heard a voice that could only have come from Fanny. Had they watched?

If so, they would now see him die. Fanny screamed something while Mama got closer.

Matthias turned around. Mama was holding something over her head. Fanny screamed again and came so close that Fips could see her—at least for a moment, before Matthias collapsed over him, and his skull crashed as hard as a stone against Fips's lower jaw.

Not again!

Fips wanted to gasp for air and scream out all the pain, but there was no more breath. Matthias was lying with all his weight on his chest. So instead of screaming, Fips twisted his eyes and lost consciousness.

***

It all happened way too fast to really understand. In one moment Matthias and Fips were still fighting at the bottom of the stairs. Matthias stabbed his brother, and the blood splashed the walls. It was clear who would win.

But in the next moment, Mama sprinted like a crazy Jack-in-the-box from the kitchen, swinging a hatchet over her head. It was like in the movies.

Fanny couldn't move, but her vocal cords still worked. She was a screaming moviegoer who had forgotten the popcorn.

And Mama? In a matter of seconds she had transformed herself from an inconspicuous extra into the heroine. Fanny wouldn't have believed that there was so much strength in this skinny woman. When Matthias, who sat astride his brother, had just turned half to her, she split his forehead with the axe. The blade got stuck there just like the knife in Fips's belly.

Matthias silently fell over and buried the seriously injured Fips under him. Fanny screamed again. Mama stood there silently and stared at her sons.

Fanny finally found her voice again. "What have you done, Mama? You killed him!"

Mama turned around, looked her daughter in the eye, and spoke directly to her for the first time in years: "I hope so."

***

Panting, Susan Edwards hurried down the hallway and finally opened the door at the end without thinking about what or who might be waiting for her behind it.

No one was there.

Just the empty room of a girl. On the bed lay an open teenage magazine, as Susan saw from the colorful pictures and frilly layout. Before she looked around, she locked the door. That would at least stop these maniacs for a moment. She could still hear the noises of the fighting brothers and the screeching of a

198

woman. So they were busy otherwise for now. That the boy had done that for her—or did it have nothing to do with her at all?—warmed Susan's heart. The other brother had had a knife, which was why Susan thought the chances of the younger one were rather poor. How long would it take for the others to search for her? She had to take precautions and make sure nobody came into this room so quickly.

Susan gathered all her strength and pushed a dresser against the door. The blanket slipped from her emaciated body. She remembered that she was in the room of a teenager, so there should be plenty of clothes in the closet.

There weren't too many in the end, but Susan found underwear and socks, as well as a pair of jeans and a sweater that fit her well enough. As she dressed, she winced repeatedly because the damn hook in her labia hurt. If all went well, she would soon be rid of it. She had to hold on to that thought.

Under the bed she discovered a pair of sneakers she could use if she tied them tightly enough. She even found winter clothes. This room was a real stroke of luck, and Susan did not fail to send a short prayer of thanks to heaven. It wouldn't be as simple as she had hoped, but she still had a chance. They hadn't caught her yet.

After she dressed, she opened the balcony door and peered into the snowy darkness. Suddenly she thought of the film *The Shining*, where the panicked mother lifted her son out of the bathroom window to let him slide down a big hill of snow to save him from his insane father. The mother didn't fit through the window herself.

Thankfully, Susan didn't have that problem. There was even a balcony here. However, the snowy hills below were by far not as high as in the movie. Nevertheless, they would absorb her jump. With a bit of luck, this would protect her from serious injury. If she wanted to live, she would have to take the risk. This was the only way out of the house. The only way back to life. It was worth a try. She should do it quickly, while the people downstairs were still busy killing each other.

Of course, Susan didn't know where the rest of the family were. After all, there were five siblings. Two of them were currently fighting in the stairwell, but where were the others? In the house or somewhere outside? It was impossible to know, but at least the boy had been quite sure that they could escape. He had probably not expected his brother to be home. Did that apply to the rest?

Susan only knew she had to take advantage of this opportunity as long as at least part of the family was distracted. She couldn't lose any time. She resolutely slipped into a blue anorak with colorful stripes and put on a red wool cap. She found matching gloves. When she looked in the mirror, she felt like a teenager for a moment. The outfit made her look years younger. Only the dirty, emaciated face and the greasy strands of hair didn't quite fit her new look. Never mind. Soon she would be able to dress the way she wanted. And she would keep stuffing herself with tasty things until she felt sick. Life and freedom were waiting for her, but she would only get this special gift if she made an effort. In this world, nothing fell into your lap.

Susan breathed deeply and stepped onto the icy balcony. She had never seen real snow, let alone touched it, except on TV and in pictures, but she was already fed up with it.

Please, dear God, give me a good landing! No fractures! If I break a bone, I'm dead.

Simple fact.

Susan trembled all over as she swung her legs over the railing. She had been athletic and in good condition all her life, but the last months in captivity had not only weakened her but also stiffened her limbs. She'd been lying around most of the time. But now there was no time to warm up.

She stared down at the bone-white snow shining in the pale moonlight and tried to estimate how many feet the drop was. Ten? Or twelve? She'd never been good at guessing. One spot was particularly snowy. Susan slid her butt along the railing until her legs dangled directly above the pile of snow. Her cheeks were hot in spite of the cold. At least it had stopped snowing, and the sky was clear. The moon served her as a source of light.

Susan tried to prepare herself for the impact. She had to try to unroll. Hopefully, her strained bones would be able to keep up.

In the end, she closed her eyes and let herself fall.

***

The moment Susan Edwards let herself fall into the pile of snow under the balcony, Peter and Andi Koller entered the house. Their heated and stressed faces collapsed as they saw the brothers, covered in blood, lying on the floor in the entrance area.

Both opened their mouths. Peter lowered his hand with the rifle, not seeming to know what to aim for. The boys looked like the losers of a bloody battle. Mama and Fanny knelt with them and held their heads on their laps.

"What the hell …" Peter started as Fanny let go of Matthias's head.

She jumped up and ran to him. "Mama killed him!" she screamed. Totally hysterical and somehow incomprehensible. Mama had killed *who*?

Andi realized Matthias was dead. A hatchet was stuck in his head. And Fips? He still seemed to be breathing, but it didn't look good.

"What the fuck happened here?" Peter roared. He lifted the rifle again, but he had no target so far.

"Fips tried to free the woman," Fanny cried.

Andi could hardly understand her.

"Matthias wanted to stop him. Then suddenly Mama came and she … she …" Sobbing, she tried to hug her father, but he pushed her away and aimed—at Mama.

You can't let that happen! a voice screamed in Andi's head.

"Is that true, wife?"

Mama slowly raised her head. She was tearstained and covered in blood. Was she mourning? For Fips? Until recently, Andi wouldn't have believed she was capable of such an emotion. But she had killed Matthias—her own son—to save her youngest. That was more than a damn emotion!

Andi felt a sting in his heart, and this once so meaningless word—*Mama*—suddenly felt warm and alive. He looked at her, and she returned his gaze. At this moment, her tear-filled eyes were no longer dead and empty but full of love and awareness.

The next second she had no eyes anymore because Dad blew her skull away. Andi gave a horrified scream. Fanny did the same. Dad laughed. Mama's head looked like a bloody plate. Most of it was spread out on the floor, along with her brains. With a dull thump she landed next to Fips on her missing face.

"Oh God! Oh my God!" Fanny screamed.

Dad turned to her, and for a terrifying moment Andi thought he would shoot her too. Instead, he lowered the rifle and nodded.

"Stop the blubbering. We have to find this bitch! It's enough that Mitzi's gone."

"Mitzi didn't run away," Fanny said almost inaudibly.

Andi pricked up his ears. "What?"

"Matthias killed her. In the hut."

"Oh my God." Andi pressed his hands against his mouth. This was just too much.

But Dad only laughed. "Wonderful. One problem less. If we had only known that right away, huh, Andi?"

Andi couldn't answer. There was a thick, aching lump of ice where his heart had been beating recently. If only he'd done something earlier! Why had he waited so long?

"Let's go! We gotta catch that bitch!" Dad said with a snarl.

"She ran upstairs," Fanny said.

"All right. I'll check there, and you two look for her outside. She can hardly have escaped, but if she did, her footprints will give her away."

"And what about him?" Fanny asked, looking at the bleeding Fips.

"He can die here. He deserves no better."

Desperately, Andi tried to catch the dull, dying eye of his brother. *Why didn't you stay in the closet, you idiot?*

Of course he knew the reason. Fips once again wanted to play the good guy and save the girl. The boy was a hopeless case. He just couldn't help it. And that would finally cost him his life. He was still breathing, but only a miracle would save him.

Dad was already barreling up the stairs with his rifle.

"I'll go outside," Andi said to his sister. "You have to get your jacket."

"Fuck the jacket!" Fanny replied impudently. Or was it the shock? Had all this gotten to her? It seemed so, even though Andi wasn't sure what upset her the most. Mitzi's death didn't seem to affect her at all.

"Why did you and Matthias kill her? Your own sister?"

"I don't know!"

"You know why."

"Who cares? We have to find the woman before she can report us."

Andi laughed out loud. It was just too ridiculous. "Do you really think there's anything to save here?"

Baffled, Fanny looked at him. As if she had just woken up. Perhaps that was even true. Tears ran down her cheeks.

She shook her head. "We still have to find her. Right? We have to stop her!"

Andi shrugged. "Let's try!"

***

Like a wild bull, Peter Koller tore open all the doors and ran into every room, looking under the beds, in the closets, and behind the curtains.

Nothing and nobody.

There was a note in Andi's closet.

Andi! I'm trying to help the woman. Sorry I didn't stay! I just couldn't! Thanks for everything. Fips.

That couldn't be true! Damn liar!

Peter crumpled the note and kicked the closet so hard that the door ripped off its hinges and his foot hurt. Such a damned lying toad! His eldest had fucked him from front to back!

"Thanks for everything," he shouted into the empty room. "Thanks for nothing, you goddamn bastards!"

205

He threw the crumpled paper on the floor and stomped on it. "You'll pay for that, boy! I'll get you for that!"

***

Susan didn't manage to roll over, but she landed softer than she had expected: on her butt with her legs stretched out. She felt no pain. She carefully checked her knees, elbows, and ankles. Everything good? All good! If she hadn't been so afraid, she would have screamed with joy. The snow was soft and powdery, thanks to the bitter cold.

Susan quickly slid down the mountain, looking around nervously. She was at the back of the house and saw nothing but snow and some objects that were so covered in white powder that they couldn't be identified. Susan suspected it was farm equipment. Didn't matter. It didn't concern her.

Breathing heavily, she trudged to the side of the house and fumbled forward inch by inch. It was a pity the girl didn't have winter boots in her closet. Susan's feet were clumps of ice. She had to climb over some snowy stuff and stumbled over and over again, but she didn't want to leave the protection of the house. Here she felt at least the illusion of security.

Suddenly there was a deafening bang. Susan flinched and almost pissed herself. Her heart kept beating in her throat. What was that? A gunshot? In any case, it had come from the house. Now she heard voices and a scream or a cry.

I gotta get away from here!

Susan held her breath. The noises in the house continued. When she came to a window and saw the light, she ducked and crawled on all fours. Whatever was going on in there …

I gotta get away or I'll die!

Was the shot fired at the boy who had tried to help her? Or was he already dead? Basically, it didn't matter what had happened to him. He would no longer be able to help her, that much was certain.

Susan had reached the corner and continued crawling. In the last moment she saw the stairs that probably led to the cellar. She would have fallen down the icy, snow-covered steps by a hair's breadth, perhaps breaking her neck, at least a leg. That would have been it.

It couldn't end like this! She hadn't come this far for nothing!

Susan crawled in a wide circle around the cellar steps and back to the house wall. She was afraid that someone might see her through a window. Then maybe the next gunshot would be for her. She barely noticed that her hands were as numb as her cheeks. *Go on, don't stop.* She could make it!

Susan finally reached the front of the house. Risky, but there was a road here, even if it was nothing more than a somewhat broader path. Had it been of any use for her to fall into the thicket behind the house in these harsh conditions? Maybe they wouldn't have found her there, but she would have died anyway. Instead, she had to try to fight her way through the forest within sight of the path. After all, it wasn't just about running away but about arriving somewhere. Susan knew she didn't have enough strength left to fight her way for hours through an unknown forest area at night in below-zero temperatures. Maybe it wasn't as remote as she thought—after all, it wasn't as vast here as in America—but the risk was still too high.

She wasn't out here to die like a wounded doe in the thicket, but to survive.

As soon as she made sure no one was in front of the house and the main door was closed, she got up and sprinted toward the road.

***

When they stepped out of the door, they saw her disappear into the woods across the street with Mitzi's colorful anorak and red cap.

"There!" Fanny shouted in excitement and pointed with her finger. "We have to go after her!"

Andi grabbed her by the arm and pulled her back so brutally that she stumbled and landed on her knees.

Completely perplexed, she looked up at him. "Are you crazy?" She tried to get up, but Andi pushed her back. "Are you totally stupid?! What are you doing? Dad will ..."

"Let her go."

"What?"

"Let her go."

Fanny jumped up and wanted to run again. Andi held her firmly. Fanny screamed and tried to break away, but Andi was stronger. He held her as effortlessly as a stubborn puppy and didn't let all that and wriggling disturb him.

"Dad!" she screamed at the top of her lungs. "Dad! He let her get away!"

And there he stood in front of the door, the rifle at the ready and his eyes casting lightning. "Let her go," the crazy old man ordered. "I know what you did."

Andi let go of Fanny, who immediately jumped over to her father like a rubber ball and, in doing so, laughed triumphantly. "She ran into the forest there, Dad."

"We'll get her," Dad said with a stoic calm that didn't match his frenzied eyes. "First I take care of this one. There was a note in your closet, Andi. From Fips."

Andi swallowed hard. The little one had once again meant well, so he didn't blame him. The only culprit here was the psychopath with the rifle, which was pointed at Andi's head.

"So you helped him," Dad stated with disappointment.

"Of course I did," Andi replied coolly. "He was the only one in this family with a spark of decency."

"You're not even sorry that you stabbed your own father in the back?"

"The only thing I'm sorry for is that I didn't do it much sooner."

The corners of the old man's mouth twitched. He raised his eyebrows, released the safety catch of the rifle. "Now you'll die!"

Andi nodded. Suddenly, he wasn't afraid anymore. Chances were quite good that the woman would make it. In any case, her chances were better than Steffi's had ever been. It wasn't bad to die now, because the life that awaited him after everything wouldn't be worth it. He was too old to pass as a victim and too young to spend the rest of his life as an outlaw.

It was better this way.

When his father narrowed his eyes to aim better, Andi closed his eyes and didn't hear the shot that tore his neck apart.

***

Fanny screamed again. That seemed to be her new favorite pastime. It was all too much. As she watched her eldest brother bleed to death—Andi gargled like a broken waterpipe—she gradually realized there was no more Koller family. Only she and Dad were left. The lump that formed in her throat felt just like the sadness she knew from her childhood. A feeling of hopelessness and homesickness that was hard to grasp. Sometimes life was strange. Maybe she missed Mama. Or Matthias. It was hard to say. Maybe she wanted to cry for Andi, whom she had always looked up to as a little girl. Dad shouldn't have shot him. What was wrong with him?

"Get in the car!" he commanded. "Let's catch that bitch!"

Fanny didn't want to and couldn't anymore. She wanted to stay here and lie down with her dead mother. She wanted it to stop.

Oh please! Let it stop!

When she didn't move right away, Dad grabbed her by the wrist. That hurt and woke her up. Like a limp doll, she let herself be dragged to the car and kept looking back at her brother, whose blood turned the snow red. Wasn't there some fairy tale about this? Fanny had forgotten. She just couldn't forget that she was now alone with Dad. As a pair, they couldn't even be a copy of a family.

Epilogue Part 1:
Monster

They're driving around. It feels like eternity. Aimless in the end. Although there is no hope anymore to find the woman, Fanny has to get out and fight her way through the undergrowth with Dad. He doesn't care that she's not wearing a jacket. Without reacting to her whining and crying, he urges her on, deeper into the forest. In the flashlight beam, Fanny falls to her knees. Her lungs are burning, and she is terribly cold.

But Dad doesn't know any pity. Now it's as if he's hunting her. As if she were the woman from the attic.

"I can't go on," Fanny wails. She turns to her father and reaches out her arms, as if hoping he would help her.

He doesn't. Instead, he points his gun at her. Fanny wails even more. She doesn't understand it, can't understand it. She doesn't want to die.

"No, Dad! Please don't!"

Dad's face is rigid, and his eyes are expressionless. Dead.

"Dad! No!" Fanny raises her arms and sobs hysterically. She doesn't want to die.

Dad doesn't respond. He looks evil, but he has always been. Fanny remembers that she sometimes wanted to sit on his lap when she was small, but he pushed her away.

She whimpers and begs for her life, but that doesn't interest him. It never has.

He lifts the rifle, pulls the trigger, and Fanny finally doesn't have to freeze anymore.

***

Peter Koller stares at his daughter's corpse. There's absolute emptiness inside him. He feels nothing. He never has. Although ... that's not quite true. He's always felt anger, hatred, and envy. And sometimes even a short moment of satisfaction. That's over now. Everything.

He throws the flashlight next to the dead Fanny. The light shines directly on her destroyed face.

Who is that? Peter doesn't know her.

He places the barrel of the rifle under his chin and stares into the black night sky. The stars are as cold as his heart. They feel nothing; they know nothing.

He walks a few steps. Away from Fanny. Even in death he doesn't want to be close to her.

He pulls the trigger.

Epilogue Part 2:
Survivors

Susan closes the door. She wants to be alone. Just for a moment. This is her room, her life, her family. She should be happy and grateful. She should walk around with a permanent grin and live every day as if it was her last. Because she survived and is finally home again.

So many hugs and kisses. So many sweet words and sympathetic looks. She is so lucky.

Why do I feel so empty?

She sits on her bed and lets her gaze wander, sees familiar things in a new light. The worst thing is that there is actually no light at all anymore. In the beginning, the feeling was magnificent, a rush of adrenaline. She was alive and had been saved. Gradually, her wounds healed, and she waited to feel better.

She doesn't feel any better.

Instead, she keeps dreaming, night and day, of that damned attic. She feels the scratching straw and smells her own excrement. It feels like she's still there. As if that was the place where she belongs. Her therapist says it will stop, but Susan doesn't believe him. She thinks of Clara far too often. Only a little bit of her DNA was found.

Did she eat parts of her? She knows that it's possible, but she can't remember. Who wants to remember having eaten her own best friend?

Suddenly Susan flinches and touches her crotch, as she often does. She still feels the snap hook. There is only a small scar on the spot. How can such big things leave such small scars and vice versa? Susan will probably never understand. She rests her hand there for a moment. How does it feel? She doesn't know.

She only knows that she's not feeling as well as everyone—especially herself—has expected. She wanted to get her life back and start all over again, but now she hardly makes more of it than she once did in the attic of the Koller house. Sometimes Susan thinks her escape was pointless. She could just as well have stayed there to die.

Will she ever get over it? Susan's not sure. Everyone says it's normal. Something like that needs time. What do they know? Mom, Dad, and all the others—none of them has been there. None have seen, felt, and tasted what she has. Only Clara, but she's dead.

Susan wonders if she only imagined the accusing expression in the eyes of Clara's parents. They probably have the right to accuse her. Susan didn't pay well enough attention. Not for herself and not for Clara. Does she feel guilty? Oh yes. Definitely!

She can't change that. And that's the worst of it. Maybe it'll get better. Maybe she'll forget the house of monsters and the stinking attic someday. Maybe.

Susan doesn't really believe it. She knows how persistent monsters are and how hard it is to survive. Because running away is always just the beginning.

***

Fips closes his eyes and feels the warmth of the sun on his face. Somehow it's summer again. This face has scars and looks slightly asymmetrical, but it's better, much better than it was. Fips can speak properly again and eat normally. That took a while, and the worst time was when his jaw was held together by a wire. He couldn't open his mouth and was fed through IVs back then. After having his lower jaw broken a second time and patched up, the pain was hell. During the first days, Fips wished he had just died. Today he sometimes wishes that too, but not quite as often.

According to his therapist, he's making progress. He can accept what has happened to him since childhood, and insight is the first step toward recovery. He slowly understands that none of it was his fault, neither the guilt of his brothers and sisters. Even Mama was a victim. Of course, they were liable for prosecution anyway, but there will be extenuating circumstances as soon as everything Peter Koller did over the years is revealed. Already he's being called the *Monster of Bavaria*.

Fips is the only surviving family member and the most important witness. Due to her traumatization, there won't be much to learn from the American girl. Meanwhile, she has flown back home. Fips hopes she will get over it. Somehow. So that her rescue wasn't in vain. If he is really lucky, his own won't be in vain either.

When the police arrived, they first thought he was dead. Then one of the officers noticed he was still breathing. He was taken to the hospital by helicopter and had emergency surgery. The rest is history.

Apart from that, they only found corpses in the house and in the forest. Without Fips's help, the reconstruction of events would have been impossible.

After he had told them about the pigs and their tragic role in this horrific scenario, the animals were slaughtered on the spot. Human remains were found in their stomachs, just like in the stomachs of the dead. It became an open secret that the whole family repeatedly fed on the meat of the victims. Sometimes it's good for Fips to talk about it. Sometimes not.

He still can't look in the mirror. He wouldn't be able to bear it. He doesn't want to see his scars or his new face. His therapist says he's a victim, that he was mentally and physically abused all his life. That he can't be held responsible for the crimes he committed under Dad's influence because he never had a choice. She says he's not a monster.

Sometimes Fips believes her. Sometimes not. Because there are days when he feels like a monster. Deep inside. There are days when he sees the monster as soon as he accidentally—and only briefly—looks in the mirror while brushing his teeth. There are days when he's sure it's never gonna be good and everything's pointless. The therapy won't help. He'll stay in this clinic forever and never lead a normal life.

And maybe this is better.

Because of the monster.

That's how Fips is doing on bad days. His therapist says that with time, the bad days will grow fewer and fewer. He should have confidence in himself and be courageous. The monster may never go away completely, but he must realize that it's not him but only a piece of the past that no longer has any power over him.

On good days it works. Fips knows he's not the monster—and neither was Mama or his siblings—only Dad. It was always just Dad. And he's dead.

The monster is dead.

Isn't it?

Wake Up!

Short story

Wake up!

Sabrina blinked. What was so bright? It couldn't possibly be daytime again!

Wake up!

She'd rather go back to sleep. The darkness was so cool and pleasant. In the darkness, she felt like a new person.

Wake up!

With a moan, Sabrina turned on her side and blinked, although it hurt. She blinked until the world slowly took shape. It was really bright. Much too bright!

Wake up!

The voice in her head was as loud and unrelenting as a fully turned-up speaker, and it rolled through her brain like a bulldozer.

Wake up!

"Okay, okay," she mumbled with a voice that sounded old and creaky. Her throat was terribly dry!

She would much rather have stayed in the darkness, just for another moment, like Timo, who snored softly next to her.

Sabrina looked at her boyfriend, who was lying on his side with his mouth open. His warm breath smelled sour. Snot and blood had formed crusts on his face. The stubble made him look older. There was no damn wake-up call in his head. He would slumber like a baby until it was time for the next shot.

Do we have any left?

The thought was louder than any alarm clock. Sabrina got up as if stung by a tarantula. A sharp pain shot through her head into her jaw.

"Ouch!" Why did her mouth always have to taste like shit when she came down?

Next to the couch on which Sabrina and Timo spent most time of their lives was the little blue-eyed main reason for waking up—at least it should have been: two-year-old Pia.

"Hello, muffin," Sabrina said in an unpleasantly cawing voice. A sip of water might have helped, but that wasn't what she wanted.

Pia wore pink one-piece pajamas and emanated the typical smell of a full diaper. When she saw that her mother was awake, she stretched out her little arms to her.

Although her arms hurt, Sabrina lifted the little one onto the couch. The child smelled even worse than Timo, who hadn't changed his blotchy boxer shorts for half an eternity. Not that Sabrina's panties were much better.

Pia's sticky hair smelled like Maggi *(Translator's comment: A liquid seasoning popular in Germany)*. When had Sabrina bathed her last? At the moment she couldn't even remember when she herself had last used the bathroom. This damned couch had become her island in a sea of garbage. When was the last time they had slept in the bedroom? That must have been weeks ago.

The couch was just more comfortable—and so practical because everything was within easy reach.

Sabrina let her eyes wander over the hopelessly cluttered coffee table. Everything on, underneath, and around it looked like a garbage dump: beer bottles, empty or half full; leftover food spilling off plates; overflowing ashtrays; used syringes; charred spoons; lighters; and trash. In between were empty and full milk bottles, cheap plastic toys, pacifiers, nibbled biscuits, and bowls with encrusted and moldy pap leftovers. The blackish-brown liquid in the baby bottles no longer resembled the milk that had once been in them.

Sabrina had woken up much too late. Meanwhile, Pia cried, and it sounded hoarse and suffocated. Sabrina took her in her arms. The small, warm body trembled.

"Shh," Sabrina said. "Shh, my little muffin. Everything will be fine."

While she comforted her daughter, she looked at the television, which was on around the clock. *The Simpsons*. Sabrina had watched this series in her own childhood. Now she was grown up, while Lisa, Bart, and Maggie were still children. They would stay kids forever. But it was always said that nothing lasted an eternity.

Sabrina looked at her boyfriend again. He would still sleep for hours, and nothing would wake him.

There were no admonishing voices in his head. Sabrina envied him. She would have rather stayed in bed, hiding in the soothing darkness until it was time to shoot up her veins again. And again the question was whether the stuff would still be enough. The little bit in the sachet on the table didn't look like it. Sabrina would probably have to go outside afterward to buy some. Fortunately, they still had some money.

Groaning, she rose with the sobbing child in her arms and made her way to the kitchen through ankle-deep garbage. It looked just like on the coffee table here, maybe worse. With one hand Sabrina pushed dirty dishes aside and struck the flies she startled with her actions. Pooh, what a stench!

Some of the plates were filled with little worms and insects, which Sabrina didn't pay any further attention to.

Wake up!

Oh yes, she should have done that …

Pia got too heavy, so Sabrina put the crying girl down. Leftover food encrusted the front of her pajamas, and snot stuck to her face. Sabrina didn't know how long the child had been left to herself. Sometimes the darkness lasted quite long.

She could still be proud of herself, because if it were up to Timo …

"Where are the damn bottles?" Sabrina desperately pulled open all the cupboard doors, but there were no clean dishes. She would have to wash something.

Unfortunately, all sorts of critters were frolicking on the piles of dishes in the sink. Nobody had cleaned here for a long time. Swearing, she reached for a baby bottle of moldy chocolate milk and had to gag when she unscrewed it. Black mold had eaten its way into the nipple.

Sabrina poured the stinking contents over the dirty plates, turned on the water, and let it run into the bottle and nipple. The mold didn't go away, but Pia's screaming had become so deafening that she had to do it quickly. It had all worked out better before, but that had been before Timo had returned. How long had that been? Sabrina only knew that Pia had still been a baby. Although Timo hadn't shown up a single time during her pregnancy, he suddenly acted like a father if he felt like it. He cuddled with Pia and said lovely things to her, which made Sabrina think of the past when he had sometimes done so with her.

Today she was only a means to an end, but what bound her to him didn't have much to do with love. And all that because of the damn heroin!

Previously Sabrina had only smoked the heroin, but after Timo had given her the first shot, she had acquired a taste for it. On a high you always felt exactly what you needed. If the reality was dark and cold, you got a lot of warmth and sunshine. And if you had enough of the sweat-inducing heat of everyday life, the jag was like a cool, dark cloth under which you could hide until everything looked better again.

Only, that didn't happen. It never got better. The more often you dived into it, the more painful the awakening. At the beginning of her pregnancy, Sabrina had undergone rehab and actually managed to abstain—unless you counted the few joints and lines that she'd needed to avoid going crazy. But then this motherfucker had returned from nowhere into Sabrina's life, and within a very short time he had ruined everything she had built up with so much effort. She had been a good mother, but he had taken that away from her. Like everything else.

Sabrina opened the fridge and gave a frustrated groan. No milk. And the filthy thing didn't really offer much if you didn't want to feed your two-year-old daughter moldy cheese and beer.

Sabrina looked at the crying Pia and shrugged. "I'm sorry, muffin. We have to go shopping."

Of course, Sabrina knew this wouldn't happen. The only thing on the list today were fresh drugs.

Pia kept sobbing. She probably hadn't eaten for days. But that was okay as long as you drank enough. At least Sabrina thought she'd read that somewhere. A human could survive for quite a long time without food. You only needed enough liquid. Did that also apply to children? Probably.

With trembling hands, Sabrina searched the chaos on the counter until she found the box of cocoa. She grabbed a spoon that looked reasonably clean and scooped brown powder into Pia's bottle. Half of it missed the vial, and it took a while until it was finally filled to three-fourths. It couldn't be sweet enough for children, and the sugar would satisfy the hunger of the little one. At least Sabrina hoped so.

She filled the bottle with lukewarm tap water, screwed the lid shut, and shook until the powder was mixed.

Little Pia stared at the bottle with big wet eyes. Greed was written all over her face, and Sabrina involuntarily thought of a hungry predator. But this was just a little girl—her own daughter—about to starve.

Wake up!

Oh yes, it was about time.

Sabrina handed her the bottle. Pia grabbed it with her dirty hands and pushed the moldy nipple into her mouth. She drank greedily and made noises that sounded almost like suffocation, as her little body was still shaken by sobs.

Sabrina watched her for a moment when a stabbing pain suddenly shot through her abdomen. Groaning, she bent down and held her bloated belly. Since she'd been on drugs again, she often had problems with her stomach and intestines and was constantly bloated, but the cramps had never been this bad. If she didn't make it to the toilet quickly, she'd probably shit her pants. In a crooked posture and with both hands on her belly, Sabrina schlepped to the bathroom.

It didn't look any different here than the rest of the apartment. Whoever had been to the toilet last—Sabrina couldn't remember—hadn't flushed.

The stench drove tears into her eyes. A swarm of black flies came out of the toilet bowl as she approached. That wasn't just shit in there. It was alive!

Sabrina pressed a hand over her mouth. Her eyes bulged out like one of those stuffed animals that her daughter loved so much. The next cramp followed and forced her to her knees. Startled vermin—flies, small bugs, and squirming maggots—crept around on tiles that were smeared with excrement and urine.

Sorry to disturb you, Sabrina thought woozily.

She gagged dryly, which made the pain even worse. Breathing heavily, she pulled herself up on the edge of the bathtub. What now? It was impossible for her to sit on this toilet! The bathtub was anything but clean, but at least no critters crawled around in it. Moaning, Sabrina pushed herself over the edge and for a moment remained lying and writhing like a fetus, while she was breathing heavily. The pain was hell. She hadn't eaten for ages—at least not that she could remember. When she was stoned she didn't need anything, and in between she had eaten mostly liquid food. Timo didn't care much, but his stock of alcohol was always visible.

Her face was contorted with pain when Sabrina took off her panties and forced herself into a squatting position. The cramps flared up again and eased a little shortly afterward.

Sabrina pushed. She hardly noticed that she was peeing and that warm urine was running over her feet. Her face was red like a tomato, and a blue vein pounded her forehead like a malformed worm.

Damn, that hurts so much! Why can't the shit just come out?

There was a good chance that she'd caught something. Not necessarily a surprise considering the unhygienic conditions. And hadn't Pia recently vomited and suffered from diarrhea? Yes, she shit all over the couch and had made Timo angry, so he had beaten her with a shoe until her back was blue like a Smurf.

Sabrina had been so sorry that she needed the next dose so quickly. Pia's whimpering sounded almost like laughter when Sabrina was high, and it looked kind of funny how Timo dragged the little girl through the apartment by her hair. How long ago was that? Days? Weeks? Anyway, it seemed plausible to Sabrina that she had been infected by Pia. Such a gastric flu could be fucking nasty. She hated that and wished for nothing but the next shot. Not that she had ever wished for anything else since the addiction had her under control again.

Sabrina pressed with all her strength. At that moment something in her gave way, and there it flopped out of her, warm and wet. That was really the load of her life. Sabrina wavered. For a second she became so dizzy that she almost tipped over. The cramps had subsided, and that was the most important thing.

Where does all this shit come from? Sabrina wondered. She'd never seen a turd like that before. It must have been the virus. She was really sick. Luckily, Timo was still asleep. He wouldn't have been happy about the mess and would have made her look like a Smurf. Sabrina absolutely had to clean as soon as she was better again. For now she was just happy that the pain had subsided. Maybe she would even be able to sleep a little.

Sabrina tried to climb out of the tub when suddenly everything around her turned black …

***

Wake up!

Again with this blinking, and the much too bright light. Was that a déjà-vu?

Sabrina rubbed her eyes. Timo sat on the edge of the couch and tied his arm while he stared at the TV.

"Timo?"

He turned around. Sabrina saw the syringe in his hand. Immediately her heart was beating. *Was it still enough?* If it had been enough for him, there would be nothing left for her! The thought made Sabrina's pulse race. She vaguely noticed that her tummy still hurt. But it had gotten better since she'd been to the toilet.

Toilet? In her life situation there were many elastic terms like this. What had actually happened? She couldn't remember how she'd gotten back on the couch.

She watched the needle disappear in Timo's swelling vein. Her own arms were so damaged that she had to inject into her feet. You could literally feel Timo relaxing. He put the syringe on the coffee table and leaned back. His hair tickled Sabrina's naked toes.

"Rolf was here," he said.

Sabrina felt an overwhelming sense of relief. Rolf was one of their dealers.

"What about you?"

Sabrina shrugged with irritation. She was not used to Timo asking about her condition. "Why do you ask?"

"Do you have your period?"

Why was he asking? Sabrina had already feared that he'd seen the mess in the bathtub and would be angry. At least he would be peaceful for the next few hours

228

now that fresh heroin was pumping through his system.

Why did he think about her period? Sabrina looked down at herself and gasped in shock when she saw the blood. Her bare legs were encrusted up to her ankles with it, and she had left ugly rusty red marks on the couch for which Timo would certainly have punished her if he hadn't been too busy with his stuff. But that was probably only postponed. If she couldn't get the couch clean again, Sabrina had to prepare herself for consequences later on. Why hadn't she noticed that? She hadn't used tampons or sanitary pads. She wasn't even wearing panties. Was that the reason for the abdominal pain? Sabrina couldn't even remember when she'd had her last period.

"The rest is on the table," Timo explained. It was typical for him that he had not immediately prepared a syringe for Sabrina. This guy really only thought of himself!

"Where's Pia?"

"She was a pain in the ass. I spanked her butt and locked her in the bedroom. Can't you hear her?"

There was actually a soft whimpering that Sabrina hadn't even noticed before.

"Why are you always so mean to her?"

"The brat is annoying! What am I supposed to do? If you would take better care of her, I wouldn't have to be so strict!" Timo's voice became softer, the words drawn out. Soon he would be completely spaced out.

Sabrina thought she should clean herself and use a tampon. She thought she should look after her child

229

and clean the couch. Besides, her stomach ached again—or still? Maybe she had to go to the toilet once more, but which toilet? Haha.

Pia's whimpering sounded weird. Hopefully Timo hadn't gone too far.

She was supposed to check on the little one and take care of her. That was a mother's job. On the other hand, she didn't want to oppose Timo. He had decided Pia had to stay in the bedroom, so Sabrina should respect that. She could look after her later. As long as she could still whine, it was certainly not so bad. Timo always said that.

In the end, Sabrina stayed on the couch again, on her island, and she only crawled to the edge to get her shot ready. Timo didn't react to her anymore. His half-open eyes were rolled upward, spittle hanging from his mouth. There was a report on television. Sabrina saw children who were doing well and mothers who cared …

It took her a while to find a suitable vein. At first it hurt, but then the sweet poison flooded her system and made her forget all the pain. The whimpering became quieter and softer until Sabrina could no longer hear it. She lay down next to her boyfriend and closed her eyes. The high deceived her with a feeling of warmth and security that she had never received or given in real life. Everything felt right and clean. And while the terrible whimpering became louder and louder in reality, it turned into a joyful laughter in Sabrina's intoxicated world of wonders. The carefree laughter of the happy child that she had never been herself and that Pia would never be.

***

Wake up!

Pia was still very small in Sabrina's dream. She held her in her arms and gave her a bottle because she was a good mother. She had banished Timo from her life forever, which was good because this man had poisoned her. In every way.

But now Pia was here and everything would be fine, even if the doctors said that she was much too small and suffered from withdrawal symptoms. Sabrina didn't think that Pia was too small. She was a perfect baby with big cheeks and round, saucer-shaped eyes. It could have all kinds of causes that she cried a lot. The only important thing was that she kept Timo away from her.

Then she received this WhatsApp message: *I am so sorry.*

Only these four words. Sabrina could have easily ignored them. After all, she knew they were as empty as the heart of the man who had written them. She could have pretended nothing had happened and could have continued to take care of herself and her little daughter who deserved it, by God.

Instead she replied: *What do you mean?*

And fate took its course, as it always did when you made the mistake of reaching out a finger to poisonous people. They wrote back and forth a few times, and then Timo called and two days later he moved in again. And of course he didn't come alone. He had plenty of poison with him and only needed a few hours to get Sabrina addicted again—and not just to the drug.

Wake up!

And she had woken up. Again and again. Every damn day, no matter how hard it was for her. She woke, got up, took care of her child. But it got harder, the intoxication lasted longer and longer, and sometimes it took days until Sabrina was really awake again.

She did not notice what happened to her daughter during this time. The screaming could be ignored and so could the stench of diapers full of poop. Sometimes Timo got upset and took his anger on the kid. The slapping of his big hand on Pia's tiny body could also be ignored.

Now and then Sabrina pulled herself together, woke, got up, took care of the child and the household. She changed diapers and prepared bottles. Just like a normal mother.

But the intervals became longer, the intoxications became deeper. Nevertheless, Pia grew up and made progress. One day she stopped crawling and ran through the apartment. Timo found it funny to knock her over. He laughed like a lunatic, but Pia didn't give up. She always stood up again and kept walking. Such a strong little girl. Sabrina was proud of her. She felt love and affection, something warm in her chest and belly, but she could not hold on to it. The addiction had her in its grip and just wouldn't let go, like a nasty little dog who had bitten its teeth into you. Sabrina really fought in the beginning. In the beginning …

Unfortunately, she overslept again and again, didn't wake up in time, and couldn't fight her way out of this damn swamp. Then Timo *took care* of the little one, who looked more and more like a Smurf. And not only did he beat Pia—which would have been bad enough—but he mocked and tortured her by putting dirty diapers on her head, knocking her over, or eating in front of her without giving her anything.

Sabrina did not understand how a man could be so cruel. Pia was just a little girl who had done no harm to anyone. For Timo, she was the target for his aggressions and his sadistic temper. At some point she didn't even scream anymore when he hit her, which Sabrina found scary. She knew it from experience. This happened when you gave up.

Wake up!

If only that wouldn't be so hard.

The whimpering from the next room sounded as if Pia was a baby again. Which was impossible.

Wake up!

If only it hadn't hurt so much.

Sabrina opened her eyes. The bluish flickering of the television was the only source of light. Her abdomen hurt. Timo lay next to her and didn't seem to have moved. Even the line of spittle on his mouth was still there, now dried.

The whimpering sounded again. Did that really come out from the bedroom?

Wake up!

"What the fuck? I'm awake!"

Sabrina struggled to get on her feet. Was this whimpering really real or was it just in her head? There was a wet spot between her legs. Fresh blood? She had to go to the bathroom but didn't want to. She had to look after Pia first. The poor girl sounded like Timo had hurt her pretty bad.

Sabrina staggered to the closed bedroom door and turned the key in the lock. Suddenly everything was absolutely quiet. No more whimpering. Since her eyes didn't want to get used to the darkness, she turned on the light. This room was hopelessly littered, just like the others. It smelled musty.

"Pia?" Sabrina took a few steps inside, climbed over dirty diapers and empty deposit bottles. Pia lay rolled up on the bed and looked okay so far. She had put a thumb in her mouth and slept like a baby. But had she really sounded like a baby?

Wake up!

"Dammit, I *am* awake!"

Suddenly the whimpering sounded again. Sabrina turned around. She had to think of the little dog that her father had let starve before her eyes to punish her. In the end it had sounded the same. That was fourteen years ago. Impossible that this dog—a toy poodle mongrel—was here now.

From whom did the whimpering come?

Wake up!

Now, that's crazy! Or am I really still asleep?

Wasn't that the only plausible explanation?

The whimpering continued.

Sabrina decided not to listen to it any further and lay down again—after all, she knew Pia was fine—when it turned into a suffocated sobbing. What the fuck was that?

She considered waking Timo, but if she succeeded, he would only become upset and in the worst case take his anger on Pia again.

No, she had to get to the bottom of this herself.

Sabrina turned off the light and left the bedroom. In the dark hallway she paused for a moment and listened. There were the muffled noises of the television and Timo's snoring ... and then the whimpering started again. It sounded like a small animal—or a baby.

Wake up!

Suddenly the cramps in Sabrina's abdomen became so bad that she sank to her knees. She felt it running out of her. Blood! That was not her period! The shock drove her back on her feet. Adrenaline raced through her body.

Wake up!

Sabrina hurried to the bathroom.

***

The bathroom was a battlefield.

Sabrina froze in the doorway. She thought about a documentary she'd seen sometime where they showed the operations at a slaughterhouse. Sabrina had no idea why she'd watched it. Nobody should see such things, let alone work in such a place, but of course there were such people. They had to be there, or how else would the meat get into our supermarkets? Sabrina had decided on that day that she would never eat meat again, but she had not done well with it. On drugs, nobody paid attention to vegetarian nutrition in intoxication or thought of the suffering of any animals in the slaughterhouses.

In those few waking moments, when the stomach growled louder than a pig could squeal at the slaughter, one simply ate everything within reach, whether it was last week's half-rotten pizza or moldy bread. Fuck the topping.

Regardless, Sabrina hadn't forgotten the pictures. And the screams. On that day she thanked God no one had yet invented olfactory television.

Now, unfortunately, she could smell it very well. Her own bathroom was the slaughterhouse, even though there were no animals here. But there was a lot of blood and feces, probably from herself. Why was she in such pain—and that bloated belly? For weeks already.

And what had she been doing in here that was so bad that she'd just wanted to forget it and go back into the living room and lay down next to Timo as if nothing had happened?

Sabrina pressed her hands over her mouth and suppressed a retching.

Did it move?

Could it really still be alive?

Trembling, she approached the bathtub and ignored the slimy tiles under her bare feet.

There it lay in a mixture of blood and shit and struggled weakly.

The little mouth was a red blistering hole.

It was still connected to the bluish umbilical cord on which hung the slimy afterbirth like a pile of innards.

Once again, Sabrina felt like she was in a slaughterhouse.

She approached the tub—and hesitated.

Flies crept around on the baby and the afterbirth.

That's placenta, Sabrina thought. And then, as if there was any context: *Now I'm awake.*

Indeed she was. Why hadn't she noticed? The child was terribly small, certainly a premature birth, but nevertheless viable, at least still. How could she have ignored it for all those months? It had grown in her, just like Pia had. But just like Pia, she had denied and disregarded this little girl.

The whimpering began again. It had become quieter.

Sabrina looked around in a hurry, grabbed a halfway clean towel, and bent over the edge of the tub, but instead of taking the little girl in her arms, she just put the towel over it—and over the disgusting afterbirth—so that only the tiny head could be seen. The baby's sticky hair was as black as Pia's and Timo's.

Sabrina gasped for air. She trembled so much that she had to sit down. Just for a moment, very briefly.

She was awake, by God, yes, and she knew very well that the newborn needed warmth and quick care in order to survive. Maybe it was already too late. The whimpering could hardly be heard anymore and the motions under the towel became weaker and weaker. The small dark eyes looked into the void; the mouth was as red, round, and moist as before.

Sabrina's hand twitched as if she wanted to touch the little girl—*her* little girl. But in the end she didn't. It was better not to do anything. Otherwise Timo would notice and punish her badly. Pia was already too much for him; another child would be the final straw. Besides, she couldn't keep it here. It surely needed medical care. And births had to be reported, children had to be registered. They needed a name, an identity.

As Sabrina looked at the little weakly breathing creature that had grown secretly within her, she decided it could not have any identity. Timo would not understand that. She hardly understood it herself, but they had already had a child and were overstrained with it. For the little thing here, it was better to never have existed.

But it existed nonetheless—that was the problem.

With a sigh, Sabrina reached into the tub and pulled the towel over the little head. There seemed to be no more baby. And no placenta. But the whimpering started again. Flies landed on the twitching towel.

Sabrina stared at it until it no longer twitched.

She did not know how much time had passed.

When she took away the towel, the baby's eyes were closed and its mouth was still open. The little girl didn't move anymore.

Sabrina covered it again and sluggishly got on her feet. At least now she knew what was wrong with her abdomen.

When she went back into the living room, her head was completely empty. There were commercials for baby food on TV. She stared at the well-fed toddlers born on the sunny side of life. Nobody could choose that, right?

Sabrina lay down next to her boyfriend, who knew nothing of what had happened in the bathroom. Thanks to the high.

She closed her eyes and wished for one thing only: to never wake up again.

PUBLISHING

PROGRAM

www.redrum-verlag.de

SIMONE TROJAHN

WITCH JUICE

REDRUM
HORROR - CUTS

SELINA'S WAY

Psycho Thriller

SIMONE TROJAHN

REDRUM

REDRUM loves you!

REDRUM liebt dich!

Visit our facebook group now:

REDRUM BOOKS - Nichts für Pussys!

www.redrum-verlag.de

www.ingramcontent.com/pod-product-compliance
Lightning Source LLC
Chambersburg PA
CBHW031947240626
47153CB00003B/886